SECRETS

MARY PETERSON

PAGE PUBLISHING, INC.
Conneaut Lake, PA

First originally published by Page Publishing 2021

ISBN 978-1-64628-499-3 (pbk)
ISBN 978-1-64628-500-6 (digital)

Printed in the United States of America

To my mom, my biggest cheerleader and toughest critic, until we meet again, I love you

Thank you for the
support!
Mary Peterson

1

DETECTIVE BRAD HASTINGS spent a little over a month in the hospital. With the beating he took, the brain swelling, and the recovery process, he was elated on the day they said he could go home.

"Well, Brad, it looks like it's time to say goodbye to you," Nurse Stevens said. "We wish you all the best and hope we don't see you any time soon. No offense," she said as she winked at him.

"None taken. I'm damn happy to be getting out of here and on with my life."

"Now, Brad, you know what the doctor said. You need to take it easy for another few weeks. After all, you did get shot and beaten," his wife, Lynda, said.

"Don't remind me. I still can't believe those punks came into the house and did that to me. If I ever get my hands on them, I'll kick their asses. I'm just glad it was me at home and not you when it happened."

"You'll do no such thing. You'll arrest them and put them behind bars where they belong. I shudder to think what would have happened if I had been home alone."

"I can't imagine what would have happened to you. I can't even think about it. I do want to talk to Nate when we get back home about a security system."

"That's a great idea, honey, but we could always move. I just hate the idea of living there after what happened. I've been staying with Sarah since then because I am too afraid of them coming back."

"I'm sorry, sweetheart. I know it's been rough on you too. I'm just grateful that Sarah had the space for you to stay there while I've been in here. I think if we get a security system, the likelihood of this happening again is very small. I'm still not sure how they knew about the safe, but I agree with Sarah. It's time to put that stuff in a safe deposit box."

"I've already taken care of it, honey. You don't worry about anything except getting back to 100%."

Nurse Stevens wheeled him to the exit of the hospital where they said goodbye and Brad and Lynda drove home.

2

WHEN THEY ARRIVED at the house, there was a Challenger parked in the driveway, so they knew that Sarah was there, waiting for them. *What a relief that someone is here*, thought Lynda. *This is the first time both of us have been back since it happened.* Sarah was Detective Sarah Wheeler, Brad's partner and stepdaughter. The day she found out they would be partners was the same day that someone had broken in to their house, beat him severely, ransacked the house, and then shot him. She had been working the case since he had been in the hospital. Once Brad had come out of the coma, he was fuzzy about the details of what happened. The doctor said that he might not remember at all because of what they did to him. All the evidence they had collected was gone through with a fine-tooth comb, trying to ID the criminals.

Even though they didn't know who had done it yet, she wasn't giving up and continued to work on it every day.

Brad and Lynda walked up to the door, and before they could open it, the door was thrown open, and Sarah stood there, beaming.

"Welcome home, Brad. Welcome home, Mom."

Startled by the door opening, they both flinched a little; but when they saw that it was Sarah, they breathed a sigh of relief, smiled, and walked into the house. They both stopped short when they entered the foyer. Each of them took in the sight of the house that they hadn't been in for over a month.

Lynda sucked in her breath and exclaimed, "Sarah! What happened in here?"

"What do you mean, Mom?" she asked, the grin on her face fading.

"I mean, it's spotless, and everything is back to where it was. Who, what, did you…" her voice trailed off as the grin reappeared on Sarah's face, only bigger this time.

"I took care of everything. The house has been cleaned, fixed, and is good as new. I even had Nate install a security system. I don't know all of the technical stuff on what he's installed, but he will be more than happy to go over it with you."

Just then Nate came into the living room and smiled and said, "Welcome home, you two. I will be happy to go over it with you once you're all settled in. If you want to wait until tomorrow, Sarah knows how to arm and disarm it, but I'm sure you will want to change the password. I've also installed a handful of cameras around the perimeter of the home, and we've put all of the equipment in the basement. The monitors for your cameras are mounted…"

"Nate," Sarah said, "why don't we let them get settled a little bit and come back in a couple of hours. Would that work for you guys?"

Lynda felt like her head was spinning around like a top.

"Um, yeah, a couple hours would be fine, I think."

"What's the matter, Mom?"

"Nothing, I just can't believe that you've done all of this. I'm overwhelmed with gratitude."

"Aw Mom, it's ok. I knew you didn't want to come back, and I knew that I wasn't going to let you come back to a house that was trashed, so I took care of it. I also didn't think that Brad needed to come home to that scene. The security system was the captain's idea, and of course, Nate said he would take care of it."

"You two have really brought some piece of mind, to me at least," said Brad.

"To me as well," agreed Lynda.

"We are very glad. Get settled, take a nap, whatever you have to do but relax. Shoot me a text when you want us to come back and walk you through the security system."

"Oh, honey, we can't thank you enough," Lynda said through tears.

"That's for sure," Brad said a little glisten in his eye.

"No worries! I'm just glad you're finally out of the hospital, Brad. It's been a little lonely at the station without my partner," Sarah replied.

"Not for too much longer. Doc says I should be able to go back in a couple weeks."

"I will be looking forward to it too."

"Me too," Brad agreed.

"Well, we're off. Let me know when you want us to come back and go through this," she said as she showed them how to arm the alarm system before they left.

3

Sarah and Nate left and were headed back to the station when Nate said, "I'm starving. Do you want to grab a bite to eat?"

"I could eat," Sarah replied.

"Ok, you pick. Anything is good with me."

So she drove to her favorite pizza place, Mountain Mike's, for lunch.

"I could eat pizza for every meal of the day," Sarah stated.

"Every one? Even breakfast?"

"Well, maybe not breakfast unless, of course, it was breakfast pizza, then yeah, I could eat it," she laughed.

"Amazing," he laughed.

"What's so funny?"

"That you could eat pizza for every meal. There are so many other wonderful choices out there."

"There are, but I really like pizza. It's quick, easy to eat on the go, and I can put anything on it I want."

"There is something to be said for being able to customize your food, I guess."

They ordered their lunch and sat, talking about Brad being home finally.

"It seems like he's been gone for so long," Sarah said.

"Yeah, it really does. I'm glad he's back. I'm also glad that you have your regular partner back."

"You said a mouthful there. Working with a temporary partner is hard. You don't know them as well as your own. Granted, mine is my stepdad, and I know him pretty well, but I'm guessing once we actually start working together, I'll get to know him even better, and that's something that I'm looking forward to."

"It gives me peace of mind knowing that Brad will be with you to protect you."

"Hey, I'm pretty good at protecting myself. I've been through a lot already in my life, and I don't need someone to protect me," she said vehemently.

"Hold on," he said with raised hands. "I'm just saying that I'm glad that your partner is someone that loves you and would do anything for you. I know you can protect yourself. I was there when that lunatic was stalking you, remember? I'm the one that got knocked on the head, but nothing happened to you except that he scared you. Apparently, I need the partner."

"I'm sorry. I just don't feel like I need protection. Yes, Brad and I will be better partners than me and someone else because we do have that bond, but regardless of our past, any partner that you have on the police force should be willing to 'go to the matt for you,' so to speak."

"I get that, but I'm still glad it's Brad and not some rookie detective that thinks he can do everything."

Their food came, so they ate and chatted about nothing.

"Ready to go back to the station?" Sarah asked when they had finished eating.

"No, but I guess we have to."

"Yeah, I've got some cold-case files I've been looking over since Brad's been gone. I might actually take them home and go through them. I don't seem to find enough time in the day to really go over them when I'm at work. We're still waiting to see if we have a match on any of those fingerprints that we sent to the FBI's IAFIS. I know our case is not at the top of the list, but it's been over a month."

"It takes time. It's not like it is on TV—one hour later you've arrested and convicted the scumbag. I just wish there was some clue as to who these guys were." Nate grabbed the bill as they got up to leave.

"You don't have to pay for lunch, Nate, I can get it."

"Nonsense. I asked you to lunch, I pay. When you ask me, you can pay."

"Is that how it works? I guess I won't be asking you out to eat, ever." She laughed at his expression. "You should see the expression on your face," she said, still laughing.

"What's wrong with my face?"

"Absolutely nothing," she stated as she leaned in and kissed his face.

"Well, if that's what happens when I buy lunch, would you like to go out for dinner?"

4

WHEN THEY ARRIVED back at the station, there was a message on her desk to go in and see the captain.

She walked over to his office, knocked on the door, and asked, "You wanted to see me, Captain?"

"Yes, Wheeler, come on in and have a seat."

She went in and sat down. He got up, walked over to the door, and shut it.

"What's going on?"

"Well, I want to talk to you about Brad. How is he doing? Do you think that he wants to come back to work?"

Relieved, she said, "Brad seems fine. I was there this morning when he came home from the hospital, and he seemed in good spirits. He was really happy with the security system, so thank you for that. I think he is really ready to come back to work. The doctor told him that he has to take it easy for the next few weeks, but I know he's chomping at the bit to get back out there. Why are you asking me, though? Why not ask Brad?"

"I wanted an honest answer. If I asked him, of course, he's going to tell me he wants to come back and right away. I'm glad they accepted the security system so willingly. But I suppose when you almost get killed, it's better to have one than not. What do you think about him being on desk duty when he comes back at least for the first couple of weeks?"

"No, he wouldn't like that at all. What about if I give him some of his cold-case files to look over while he's home? It will kind of ease him back into the swing of things. Since he won't have to take new cases until he comes back, maybe something will jump out at him, something that might have been missed earlier. Having to not take new cases might help too. He can concentrate on one at a time."

"Say, that's not a bad idea. When are you going over there again?"

"I'm just waiting for them to text me that they want us to come back and show them how the security system works. When we left today, I told them to relax and get settled in, and then Nate and I would go back over and show them how it worked. Nate can tell them all the technical stuff I know nothing about."

"Ok, that sounds like a good idea. Pick out a couple of files and bring them with. One other question, but this is about you. How are you doing? Things seem to be getting serious with Nate."

"Things aren't that serious with Nate, but I do like him a lot. He's been pretty terrific with everything that's happened to me and my family lately. I'm glad that you sent him to my place when that psycho was stalking me. So to answer your question, I'm just fine."

"Glad to hear it. Just remember, when Brad is back up to speed, you're going to have to switch partners again. But I'm going to go out on a limb here and say that you will be more than happy with that switch."

"You got that right! I'm looking forward to working with Brad for sure. He knows so much, and I know I can learn a ton from him. Thank you again for pairing us up."

"It was a good idea. You're bullheaded, and he's a veteran that I know you will listen to."

"Can't argue with you on either of those points. Well, I'll go get a couple of files ready for Brad, and I'm actually going to take one of them home with me as well. It's a kidnapping case from several years ago, and I'm interested to see what was done and why she wasn't found."

"Good luck with that, Wheeler. Go on, get out of here and take care of your partner."

"Will do, Cap'n."

She left his office, went to her desk, and started looking through the cold-case files that she had locked in her drawer over a month ago. No time like the present to give them another once-over to see what she would bring to Brad. She selected three files and put them on the corner of her desk so she would remember to grab them. She put the one that she was bringing home on top of those so she could take it home with her to look over and see if she could spot something that was missed.

Just then her phone chirped. It was her mom saying that if they wanted to come over for dinner, they would eat and then Nate could show them the security system. She responded with an ok then texted Nate that they would be going to her mom's for dinner and then he could show them the system. Sitting at her desk, she decided to open the file about the kidnapping.

As she read it through, she lost track of time and didn't even realize that it was almost five when Nate knocked on her desk and said, "Earth to Sarah. Hello? Are you ready to go?"

"Huh? What? Oh, hi, I'm sorry. I was going through this file, and I seem to have lost track of time. Yes, I'm ready to go."

They drove out to her mom's and when they got there were surprised to see a different vehicle in the driveway.

"I wonder who that is," Sarah said.

"It might be a friend of theirs. There is no one outside, so it must be someone they know."

"Let's hope so."

They walked up to the door and knocked. Lynda came to the door and opened it, laughing.

"Hello you two, come on in. The captain stopped by, and he's got us in stitches."

"Hey, Cap," Sarah said.

"Hey, you two. I guess I'll be going now."

"Oh, nonsense," Lynda said, "stay and eat with us. I made lasagna and garlic bread. Thanks to the magical grocery fairy, there's actually food in the house."

She turned and winked at Sarah, who in turn gave her a warm "you're welcome" smile.

"Well, if you insist."

5

THEY FINISHED UP eating, and Sarah said to Brad, "I almost forgot, I brought you some cold-case files to look over."

"Oh?"

"I asked her to bring them over, Brad. I thought it might get you back in the swing of things, and I know that you're anxious to get back to work."

"Thanks. I think this is just what I need to ease myself back."

Lynda and Sarah went into the kitchen to clean up and left the men to talk.

"Brad looks like he's feeling a lot better," Sarah commented.

"Oh, he is. I think just being home from the hospital has done wonders."

"Do you think that he will want to come back to work? You had mentioned that you guys had talked about retiring early."

"Not this early. We couldn't afford it. I'll be going back to work full-time, and if he were here by himself all day long, he would go stir crazy. Maybe in a few years we will retire, but not now."

"Ok, that's good to know."

"Why do you ask, sweetie?"

"I haven't had a chance to be his partner yet, and I know that I could learn so much from him. I'm just glad that I'll get the opportunity."

"You will get the opportunity for sure. And thank you very much for filling up our fridge and freezer. You didn't have to do that."

"I know, but would you really have wanted to come home on Brad's first day back and have to go to the grocery store? You've got other things to take care of, and having to go grocery shopping didn't need to be one of them. Why don't you go back into the living room and Nate can show you guys about the security system? I can finish this up."

"You know what? You are like the best daughter ever." She held up her hands as Sarah started to protest. "No, listen. You've been here for us through this whole rotten thing, you've been working on finding out who did this, you filled our house with food, you had a security system installed, and you made sure that the house was spotless before we came back home. I couldn't ask for a better friend than you. I'm so happy that nothing happened to you all those years ago because I don't know what I would do without you." Lynda wiped a stray tear off of her face.

"Oh Mom, I'm the lucky one. You've supported me in everything that I've ever wanted to do. You're my biggest cheerleader and my best friend. You're one of the strongest people I know. You're kind, considerate, and just a nice person. I'm the one that wouldn't know what to do without you. Everything that I went through as a kid would have crushed me if you hadn't been there for me, and I don't know if I ever did this, but I want to thank you for everything that you've ever done for me and for letting me be me. I love you."

"Oh Sarah! I love you too, and everything that you've ever gone through has made you into the wonderful woman that you are today. I appreciate you and Nate. Speaking of Nate, how are things going?"

"Things are good. I really like him, a lot."

"I think he really likes you a lot too."

"I think you might be right. Now get out there and learn your new security system."

Lynda reached out to Sarah and gave her a "mom" hug and went to the living room. When Sarah finished cleaning up the kitchen, she went to the living room as well. She walked in and noticed that the Captain had left and Nate was explaining the system. Since she'd already heard all about the security system, she sat on the couch and looked through the files that she had brought over for Brad.

6

"WELL, THAT ABOUT does it. Do you guys have any questions?" Nate asked.

"Not right now. Honey, how about you?" Brad looked at Lynda.

"No, I don't either. But if I do, I bet I know who I can call," she said with a smile.

"Of course, you can, Lynda. Anytime at all."

They walked back into the living room where Sarah sat, looking over files. Nate sat down, put his arm around her shoulders, and kissed her temple. Sarah blushed a little and leaned against him.

"What's on your guys' agenda for the rest of the evening?" Brad asked.

"Oh, not too much. I want to go home and get started on that cold-case file about that kidnapped little girl. Do you remember that one, Brad?"

"I sure do, like it was yesterday. It happened right after we moved out here. So very sad, that little girl, Jesse, was six when she went missing. Her and her mom were at the grocery store, and she was sitting in the cart. They checked out, went out to the car where her mom, Shelly, took Jesse out of the cart while she put groceries in the trunk. When she finished, Jesse was gone. No sign of her at all, except for her favorite stuffed animal lying on the ground by the passenger-side car door."

"Oh, that's just awful! When I think about what could have happened to Sarah, it gives me the chills. Did she have any idea who took her daughter?" Lynda asked.

"No, she looked everywhere, ran back in the store to see if she went back in there. She called 911 within minutes of Jesse going missing, and we never found her. She'd probably be around thirteen or fourteen years old by now, if she's still alive."

"Was there ever a ransom demand?" Sarah questioned.

"Not that was ever given to us. I think that if Shelly had ever gotten one, she would have turned it in. She was an absolute wreck. She had recently separated from her husband, Allan Sharpe, and had moved to Chico to get away from him. She told us he was abusive and that she had finally gotten the courage up to leave because he had started showing signs of abusing their daughter. We questioned him, and the Hollywood cops watched him for months but couldn't find anything on him. I still think he's responsible somehow but can't prove it, and we couldn't find a body. He lives in one of those big mansions, has all kinds of hired help who we also questioned, but no dice. His lawyer called the captain and told him that if we didn't stop harassing his client, they would sue the department. Since he lives in Hollywood, we were told that their missing-persons squad would handle it, but I never got rid of that file because I just couldn't. After helping out when Sarah went missing, I just wouldn't give up on this case. Captain finally had to tell me that we couldn't do anything about him because he was out of our jurisdiction. I still have a contact there that looks in on him once in a while, and when I say looks in on, I mean he watches him. He's never made a wrong move, but someday he will."

"What makes you so sure it was Jesse's father?"

"Call it gut instinct or intuition or whatever you want to call it, but I think that Allan did something to that little girl, and I want to prove it. Not just for Jesse but also for her mom. She needs to know if her daughter is alive or if she was killed."

"Well, I'll read it over again tonight and see what I come up with. Do you think that the captain would let me go out to Hollywood and question him?"

"Probably not, but you never know. If you think you can prove something by talking to Allan, then ask him if you can go."

"Ok. I'll look it over and see what, if anything, jumps out at me. But it's getting late, and we should be going. Thanks for dinner."

"Thank you, guys, for coming over and showing us all of this and for the company," Lynda said.

"Yes, thanks, kids, for everything. And I mean everything, everything that you did for Lynda while I was in the hospital, for visiting me, for making sure the house wasn't a disaster when I was able to come, for the food you filled up the fridge and freezer with. It's been such a great homecoming. I couldn't ask for a better family."

"Brad, I would do anything for you, you know that. Besides, Mom staying with me was ok. We got to hang out, and it was nice to be able to spend time with her when things weren't super crazy."

"Being at Sarah's really gave me peace of mind. I was so scared about what was happening with you, and she just made it easier all the way around."

"Well, I just really appreciate it all, including you, Nate. This system is state of the art, and I'm very pleased with the way you did everything. Ok, enough mushy stuff. You kids get out of here so I can be alone with my wife," Brad said, his eyes sparkling.

"On that note, yep, it's time to go. See you guys soon."

Nate and Sarah practically ran out the door.

Once in the car, Sarah looked at Nate and burst out laughing and said, "Oh my goodness. Did you see the look on his face when he said that? I'm really glad I don't live there. I'd have to move."

Nate was laughing too and said, "I know, right? That was a little bit more than what I bargained for."

7

ON THE DRIVE back to her house, Nate reminded her that his car was at the station.

"Oh, that's right. Do you want me to drop you off, or bring you over in the morning?"

"In the morning? Are you bringing me home and picking me up?"

"No, I thought you could stay at my place tonight."

"Oh, you did, did you? I think that's a terrific idea and very unexpected, I might add."

"Why unexpected? Mom's not there anymore, and I want you to stay with me, unless you don't want to?"

"Are you kidding me? Not want to? Hell, it's the only thing I've wanted since I met you. But it's not about sex. It's about being with you, holding you, talking to you without having to pick up the phone. I don't want to just stay over tonight, Sarah. I want to stay over every night. I realize you might not be there right now, but when you're ready, I want us to move in together."

"That's a very giant step, Nate. No, I'm not there yet, but I'd like to see how it goes this one night, and we can talk about it. I'm not sure if I'm ready for sex yet either, but I know I hate it when you leave. I like having you with me to talk to, to hold, and to kiss whenever I want to. I like that I can be me with you, and you like me in spite of it. I know I'm not perfect, and I will never claim to be, but I know I'm a lot happier when I'm with you. Nathan Drake, I do believe that I'm falling in love with you."

"Seriously? I can't believe you just said that! You've just made me one very happy guy."

They got to Sarah's and once they were in her apartment, Nate grabbed her and planted a long, make-you-lightheaded, passionate kiss on her.

He then got down on one knee and said, "Sarah, my life hasn't been the same since meeting you. I think about you all the time, morning, noon, and night. Every time we are together. I'm the happiest man there is, and when we are apart, I feel like part of me is missing. You've brought so much joy into my life. I know I'm not perfect either, but I do know that I love you and want to spend the rest of my life with you."

He reached into his pocket and pulled out a ring box with a one-carat marquise-cut diamond ring. When he presented it to Sarah, her mouth dropped open.

"Sarah Wheeler, will you make me that happiest man alive and marry me?"

Tears in her eyes, she pulled him to his feet and said, "Yes, Nathan Drake, I'll marry you!!" She threw her arms around him and hugged him fiercely and then started to cry.

"Hey, what's wrong?" he asked as he tilted her face up to his.

"Nothing, I'm just so freaking happy and shocked. You say some of the nicest things to me. I'm a very lucky girl, but don't you want to wait until we have sex to see if you even want to marry me? It could be a disaster, and then you'd be stuck with me forever."

"It won't be the worst sex of my life, and yes, I'd want to marry you even if it was. I'm ok with being stuck with you for the rest of my life as long as you're ok being stuck with me."

"I can't think of anyone else I'd rather get stuck with."

They kissed, and it was hot and passionate.

"Nate?"

"Hmmm?"

"Can we go to my room now, or are we going to stand out here, making out?"

"Oh, we can definitely go to your room. If for any reason you change your mind, please let me know. I want this to be special and memorable."

"It will be the most special thing that's happened to me in a very long time."

They walked to her room, holding hands. When they got to the door, Nate told her to keep the light off.

"Why, are you embarrassed to see me?"

"No, babe, how can you say that? I want to do this a little unconventionally. I'd like us to use other senses besides sight. I want to touch your entire body. I want to feel it with my hands, lips, and tongue. I want you to enjoy every aspect of this, and I'm going to do my damndest to make sure that you do. I want to give you as much pleasure as I possibly can."

"Is it hot in here? 'Cause I'm burning up."

"Well, we should take those clothes off then so you aren't so hot."

He moved closer to her and kissed her deeply. She moaned against his mouth and pressed her body to his. She could feel his arousal through his jeans, and she rubbed against it. His hands moved along her back, and then he slipped them between them to help her take her shirt off. They separated enough just to take off their shirts and were kissing again.

"Mm," he said. "You better stop that, or you won't have as much fun as I want you to," he growled sensually.

"We don't want that now, do we?" she whispered back.

He gently laid her on the bed and helped her off with her jeans. Once she was naked, he removed his clothes and, starting at her ankles, massaged her entire body with his hands, tongue, and lips.

He stopped what he was doing, and Sarah, who was breathless, sat up and asked, "Is everything ok?"

"Everything is perfect. You have the most beautiful body."

"How can you tell? It's pretty dark in here."

"Oh, I can tell, trust me. Now just lie back and enjoy yourself."

She laid back down. She moaned and tried to touch him but he wouldn't let her. He continued to caress and feel her entire body.

She was having a hard time containing herself because it felt so good. This was what she had been missing out on? Why had she waited so long? He gently played with her, caressing and touching every part of her body. She was going to go out of her mind. She didn't know what was happening to her, but oh, how she loved it. He continued kissing her and ran his hands up and down her body. Sarah moved out of his reach and told him to lie down on the bed, that it was his turn. She kissed him deeply, playfully darting her tongue in and out of his mouth while feeling his body with her hands. Since she had never done anything like this, she was unsure of what to do next. By his reaction, she was sure that she was doing something right.

"You don't have to do this, Sarah," he said a little breathlessly.

"Mm, I know I don't have to. I want to. Just lie back and enjoy it."

"Oh, I'm enjoying it, all right!"

She went back to what she was doing, and when she thought he couldn't take any more, stopped abruptly.

She looked at him in the dark and said, "I'm not sure what comes next, I mean, I do, but I don't know how to start it."

"You just leave everything to me. Here, lie down."

He took his time making love to her, and they were both completely satisfied.

"Is it like this all the time?" Sarah asked breathlessly.

"Not all of the time," he said, gasping for air. "Sometimes it's more exciting."

"More exciting? This was amazing, I don't think it can get any better!"

"Well, that sounds like a challenge to me."

"As long as it doesn't sound like something you think we're going to do tonight, you're on, but right now I just want to curl up in your arms and go to sleep."

"That sounds like a perfect idea. Oh Sarah, were you hurt?"

"Nothing I can't handle. At first it hurt, but then it was very pleasurable." She yawned and asked shyly, "Was it good for you too?"

"Baby, it was great. I'm glad that we could celebrate our engagement this way."

"Me too. I need to call Mom and let her know. But it will keep until tomorrow." She reluctantly got up to use the bathroom and put on a nightshirt. "Do you want a T-shirt to wear?"

"No, that's ok, I don't normally sleep with anything on. And honestly, I wish you wouldn't either."

"I don't normally sleep naked, but nothing we've done for the past several hours is what I normally do. Well, when in Rome." With that, she took off her nightshirt, threw it on the floor, and crawled into bed next to him where he was waiting with open arms. She snuggled in and said, "This has been the most amazing day. I love you, Nate, and thank you for being patient with me while we were, you know."

"Making love? Of course. I wanted your first experience to be one you'd remember. I love you too."

"Oh, I'll remember it, all right! Good night, honey."

"I'm glad. I'll remember it too. Good night, sweet Sarah."

They fell asleep wrapped in each other's arms.

8

WHEN SARAH WOKE the next morning, she felt like the luckiest girl in the whole world. Nate was there with his arms wrapped around her, she had a rock on her finger, she finally had sex, and it was absolutely the best feeling. There wasn't anything that would bring her down today. She rolled over and looked at Nate, watching him sleep for a few minutes before she decided to wake him up. She put her hand between their two bodies and touched him.

His eyes opened, and when he looked at her, he said, "I've created a monster! Can't get enough of me, huh?"

She smiled sweetly and said, "You've awakened something in me I didn't even know that I had. You're going to have to be the one that keeps it in check."

"I can do that."

They made love again, and it was just as wonderful as it had been the night before. She thought, *I can get used to this.*

She smiled at him and said, "Time to get ready for work," and hopped out of bed to get in the shower.

He went into the bathroom and said, "You know, you're going to have to bring me home before we go to work, right?"

"Why?"

"Because I need clean clothes. I can't go to work in the same things that I had on yesterday."

"Oh, ha, I didn't even think about that. You're probably going to want to leave some clothes over here."

"Or, you could move in with me, and we wouldn't have to have two places."

"Well, I'll have to think about that."

"We are engaged. It wouldn't be like we were 'shacking up'. We're getting used to the idea of being together before we get married. Call it a trial run."

"We're engaged. I really like the sound of that." Just then the shower curtain was pulled back, and he climbed in with her. "Just what do you think you're doing?"

"I decided we should save some water, and this way, I can wash your back for you."

"Aren't you the sweet one, worrying about my back not getting clean?"

"Yes, ma'am, I am, and I aim to please."

"I would say you have the pleasing part down." She smiled at him seductively.

"I think you should change the look on your face, or we are going to be very late for work."

"Oh fine, I'll get out so you can finish up."

She got out of the shower, toweled off, and went in to get dressed.

Nate finished his shower and, when he went to get out, noticed that there wasn't another towel around, so he called out to her, "Hey, hon, can you grab me a towel?"

"Oh yes, of course, sorry." She grabbed one out of the closet and handed it to him. She stood in the bathroom, just taking in the sight.

"Do you like what you see?"

"I love what I see. Makes me want to call in sick."

"We can't both call in, so we should just go to work."

"You are no fun."

"That's not what you said last night."

"Ha, ha. Get going, I'm almost ready. If we leave soon enough, maybe we can grab a bite to eat on the way in."

"I'll be ready in a flash." Once Nate was dressed, they headed to her car and then to his house. He ran in quick, changed, and was out before long. He tossed her a granola bar. "I don't think we'll have enough time, but this might tide you over until you can grab something else."

"You're so sweet," she said, her stomach grumbling. "Just in time too."

They made it to the precinct just in time for her to get to her desk by 8:00.

9

SINCE THERE WERE no new cases to work on, Sarah had a few minutes to herself. She thought, *I really need to let Mom, Brad, and Dad know that I'm engaged.* She texted her mom to see what time she would be home that evening. The response was that she hadn't gone to work at all that day. No showings, and she wanted to be with Brad for another day. Sarah called her and asked if it was ok for her to stop over.

"Well, of course, it's ok dear. Is everything all right?"

"Yes, just fine. I'll be there in a little bit."

She went to the captain's office to let him know that she was running over to her mom's and that when she came back, she would like to talk to him. He said fine, and she left. She decided to see if Nate wanted to come with her. She texted him, and he said, unfortunately, he was in the middle of something and couldn't get away. *Oh nuts*, she thought, *I'll go tell them myself.*

She got to her mom's, walked up to the door, and knocked. She heard a muffled, "be right there," and waited. The door was opened, and things started beeping.

"This damn alarm system, I can't figure it out," her mom said, annoyed.

"Here let me show you, Mom."

Sarah showed her what to do next time, and Lynda said, "Thanks, sweetie. Now, what brings you by?"

"Is Brad here?"

"Yes. Brad, could you come into the living room please?"

"Sarah?" Brad said as he walked into the living room. "What's going on?"

"Sarah has something to tell us." Sarah didn't say anything at all. She held up her hand, and Lynda exclaimed, "Oh my god! You're engaged? Oh darling, that's wonderful! I'm so very happy for you!"

"Well, I'll be, he has good taste. That's a beauty!" Brad said with a beaming smile on his face.

"He asked me last night" Sarah gushed. "I didn't think that this day would ever come, but I'm ecstatic!"

"Have you set a date? What kind of wedding do you want? Do you want me to go with you to pick out a dress? Where are you going to have the—"

"Whoa, slow down, Mom, we haven't talked about any of that. We got engaged last night, and we didn't talk about it again. We aren't in a big hurry to get married, so there will be time to answer all of your questions at a later date. But yes, when the time comes, I would love for you to help me pick out a dress."

Lynda beamed and said, "And of course, I will."

"Well, I wanted to share my news, but I have to get back to work."

"You're just going to come in here, drop a bomb, and leave?"

"Yep, I sure am. Bye guys, see you later. I need to call Dad and tell him too." Sarah left them staring after her as she walked out to her car.

"I can't believe she's engaged. I didn't think she would ever let her guard down enough for this to happen. I wonder how long it will be before she makes us grandparents. This is all so exciting."

"Lynda, don't get carried away. They've been engaged for less than twenty-four hours. Give them some time to get used to the idea, and then you can bombard them with questions."

"I'm not bombarding! Am I?"

"Just a little bit, honey. But I can't blame you. It is very exciting news, and I couldn't be happier for them."

"Me either. I really like Nate too. Oh, I'm so happy for them."

"Me too, honey, me too."

10

When Sarah got back to the station, she went to Layton's office to tell him the news.

His door was open, so she knocked lightly and asked him, "Do you have a minute, Captain?"

"Yeah, come on in, Wheeler. What is it?" Sarah shut the door before she sat down.

"Well, I have something to run by you."

"Oh? What does it have to do with? A new case?"

"No, not a new case, sir. I have to show you this." She reached out her left hand and showed him her newly acquired jewelry.

"What's this?" He looked at the ring and smiled wide and said, "Well, I'll be. Congratulations, Sarah. Nate?"

"Of course, it's Nate. Who else would it be?"

"I don't know, I'm just making sure. This is very good news indeed."

"Thank you. I just wanted to keep you in the loop."

"Thanks, and Sarah, I mean it, congratulations. He's a great man, and I'm glad for both of you."

"This is kind of your fault, you know."

"My fault?"

"Yeah, you sent him over to my house to install surveillance equipment, so it's your fault."

"I didn't know you were placing blame on anyone, but I'm ok with it."

"Me too. I just wanted to scare you a little bit."

"Get out of here, Wheeler," he said with a grin on his face.

Sarah went back to her desk and called her dad from her cell.

"Hello, honey what a nice surprise."

"Hi, Dad, how are you?"

"I'm fine. How are you? What made you decide to call this morning?"

"Well, I have something to tell you, and it can't wait."

"Oh, what is it? Is everything ok with your mom and Brad?"

"Yes, they're both fine. It's about me."

"Are you ok, have you been hurt?"

"No, I haven't been hurt, but Nate and I are getting married."

"What? Oh sweetheart, that's fantastic! I'm very glad you didn't make me wait any longer. Have you made any plans?"

"No, we just got engaged last night. Haven't even talked about it except to say yes. I'm so happy, Daddy!"

"My little girl is engaged. Naomi will be just as thrilled as I am! This is the best news I've heard in a very long time. Congratulations, Sarah. I couldn't be happier for you!"

"Thanks, Dad! He's pretty terrific."

"Can I tell you a little secret?"

"What is it, Dad?"

"When Brad was in the hospital and I came to visit, Nate asked me then if he could have your hand in marriage. I didn't know him very well then, but I said if Sarah is happy with you, then I will be happy with you, and I gave him my blessing."

"Are you serious? He's been planning this for that long? He is full of surprises, isn't he?"

"I would say so. Now, if you want to come shopping out here for dresses, I'm sure Naomi would be very excited to help you with that."

"We'll see what happens. How would you guys like a visit next weekend?"

"Next weekend, let me check the calendar. Hmm, yep, looks like we will be free. I'll let Naomi know to expect you guys, and we'll paint the town in celebration of your engagement."

"You don't have to go to any trouble for us, Dad. It's just nice to visit."

"It won't be any trouble. Leave everything to me. This is going to be fun!"

"Ok Dad," she laughed "you make the plans, and we'll go along for the ride. I've got to run. I just wanted to share my news. I love you, Dad."

"And I love you too, sweetheart. Take care."

"You too. Bye, Dad."

"Goodbye, honey, and congratulations again."

11

SARAH OPENED UP the case file on Brad's home-invasion case to see if anything would jump out at her. She hadn't looked at it in a few days and thought, *Maybe I'll see something this time that I haven't seen before.* She reread all the reports from that day. Something seemed out of place, but she couldn't put her finger on it. She set the file aside and checked her e-mail to see if she'd gotten word about any of the prints that were left at the scene. There was nothing in her e-mail about the case. Frustrated, she picked the file up and looked through it again. *What am I missing?* she wondered. She decided to put it down and look over the kidnapping cold case that she brought back with her that morning.

Since she hadn't had a chance to read it the night before at her place, she opened up the file and started at the beginning. It was lunchtime when she put the file down, only about three quarters of the way through it. It brought back so many memories. It was hard to go on, but she knew that if she was going to help this family, she needed to push those emotions aside and do her job.

She texted Nate to see if he wanted to go to lunch, but he told her he was in the middle of something and couldn't go. She grabbed her keys and decided to go home and see what she had to eat there. She brought the file with her, thinking she'd look it over while she ate. Once at her apartment, she heated up some leftovers and sat on the couch, reading more of the file. Brad had summed it up well. It was like he memorized every detail about that case. Sarah had a couple of questions and thought she'd run over to their house to see if he had answers. She put her dishes in the sink and headed to her mom's.

She pulled in the driveway, walked up to the house, and knocked. There was no answer. She tried the door. It was locked, thank goodness. She texted her mom and found out they had taken a short road trip just to get out of town. When her mom text to see if everything was ok, she decided to call her.

"Hello? Sarah, is everything all right?"

"Yeah, I just had a couple of questions for Brad about that kidnapping case, but it can wait."

"Are you sure? He's right here. We're just driving up toward Red Bluff just to get away."

"No, you guys enjoy your day. I'll talk to him about it later."

"If you're sure?"

"I'm sure, Mom. Thanks, and have a great day. Bye."

"Goodbye, sweetie."

Damn, she thought, *I really wanted to ask him about this, but since he's not back to work yet, I'll just write it down and ask him later.*

12

ONCE BACK AT the station, she put her thoughts down on paper and moved on to a new file when she decided to look back at Brad's file. She took the photos out and was looking at them: before and after photos, before evidence was collected, while it was being collected, and after they were done. She snapped her fingers. *That's it, that's what's missing.*

She went to Layton's office and said, "I think I found something in Brad's case. Well, not really found, but something's missing."

"Spit it out, Wheeler."

"Look at these pictures. Notice anything?"

"They're crime-scene photos, so?"

"What are they missing?"

"I don't know. I don't know the house like you do."

"Not the house itself, but what CSI did to the house."

"Sarah, just tell me please. I don't have all day to look these over."

"Sorry, I guess I'm just excited. When my place was broken into, CSI dusted almost my entire apartment, and you could see that dust everywhere. It looked like a black bomb went off in there."

"And?"

"And look at the photos of their bedroom, specifically the safe. There is no dust on it. I guess I didn't miss it the day we were there because the safe was never opened. Do you think this could be an inside job? I mean, from someone in this station?"

"What? No, I don't think that at all. Why would you say that?"

"Because if CSI had dusted the safe, Nate and I both would have had that stuff on our fingers, and neither one of us did. Someone may have overheard Brad talking about the safe here one day or whatever, but whoever did this knew it was there, and CSI never dusted for prints on the safe."

"Let me see those pictures again." She handed them to him. "Well I'll be," he said. "Whatever made you think about this?"

"I looked through the file this morning, went home for lunch, and I was actually looking over another file, and it just hit me. Maybe because I had been home and remembered what my place looked like after that experience. I don't know. But what do you think? Could it be someone from here?"

"I guess it could be. Everyone here has been fingerprinted, so if there was an unknown print in the house, it would have shown up."

"Unless it's a CSI. They wouldn't dust for their own fingerprints, especially knowing they are in the system."

"You make a valid point, Wheeler. Who was there for CSI that day?"

"Let me check." She flipped through some pages. "Zach Sanderson and Neal Jefferson," she told him.

"Nice work, Sarah. I'm glad you work for our team."

"Thanks, Cap. Mind if I go over to their house and dust the safe?"

"Not at all. If this is going to help us catch the bastards that did this, I'm all for it. If Shane isn't busy, why don't you take him? He is going to be bucking for detective soon too, and this will do him some good."

"Thanks, I'll see if he's here. I'll let you know what I find when I get back."

"Ok, don't talk to anyone else about this, just me, oh, and of course, Shane if he's here."

"Yes, sir."

Sarah left his office in search of Shane, calling her mom at the same time.

"Hi, Mom? Have you guys changed the password on your alarm yet?"

"No, dear, we haven't, why?"

"I have a theory about the break-in, and I need to get back in the house."

"Really, what's your theory?"

"I can't talk about it right now. I need to get over there and take another look around."

"Well, ok. Let us know later?"

"I will, bye," she said and hung up before she heard her mom say goodbye. She spotted Shane heading out the door and yelled, "Shane!"

"Yeah?"

"Hey, Cap asked me to take you with me."

"Where are we going?"

"Over to Brad's. I have a theory, and he wanted me to take you with since you'll be testing for detective soon."

"Sweet. What are we going to do when we get there? What's the theory?" Sarah told him what she thought, and he whistled.

"Really think it could be someone in the department?"

"I don't know. That's why we're going over there—to see if I'm on to something. Do you have a fingerprinting kit in your squad?"

"Yup, just in case."

"Ok, let's take your car."

They jumped in and headed to Brad's. Once they got there, Sarah dug out her keys, let them in, shut off the alarm, and headed upstairs with Shane. Once they got to the bedroom, she opened the closet and looked at the safe in the floor.

"Wow," said Shane, "what the hell happened to that?"

"That was beat up when the house was broken into. They couldn't get into it, so decided to try to break it. I was able to get it open, and it wasn't until today that I thought about it not having fingerprint dust on it. Ok, let's dust this bad boy and hope it tells us who did this."

"Ok, I'm on it." Shane dusted while Sarah lifted. They finished in about a half hour, taking about fifteen prints off the safe. Sarah said, "Let's hope to God that there are other prints on here besides mine, Mom's, Brad's, and Nate's."

"I'm with you on that. Let's get back to the station and run them through the system."

Sarah reset the alarm, locked the door, and they left for the station to see if the fingerprints they collected were in the system.

13

SARAH WENT TO Captain Layton's office to tell him that they were running the prints right now and had lifted about fifteen from the safe.

"I still can't believe that we all missed this before."

"To be fair, Captain, CSI is the one that is supposed to make sure nothing is missed. I didn't think about it because I was so worried about Brad, and it's taken this long for it to click in my brain."

"Well, I just hope you're right. Honestly, I hope you're not right because that means we have a criminal among us, and that pisses me off."

"I hope I am right. We can finally put this to bed, and it will be my first solved case."

"Let me know as soon as you hear anything."

"Will do." Sarah left his office and went to wait for the scans on the prints to be completed. She was at her desk when her phone rang. "Detective Wheeler," she answered.

"Detective, this is Fred. I wanted to let you know that those scans are completed."

"I'll be right there."

She stopped by Shane's desk to tell him they were ready. They headed to the office to get the results. Positive matches on thirteen of fifteen prints. Several of them were from the same person, but the one that stood out was one that should have never been there.

"The captain is not going to like this," she stated when she finished looking them over.

They walked to his office, went in, and shut the door.

"What have you got?"

"Positive matches for thirteen of fifteen prints. Several of them were repeats like mom and Brad, but Jefferson's were also on there and two unknowns. They might be Jefferson's partner. What are you going to do, Cap?"

"I'm going to call him into my office and show him what we've got. He will tell me who his partner is, or so help me. I can't believe that one of our own is a crook and against a decorated veteran at that. It really pisses me off. He's been with the department for five years or more. Ok, get out of here. I need to see if he's here today so we can have a little sit down."

"Can I be here when you do?" Sarah asked hopefully.

"Not this time, Sarah. I may not be very nice to him to get him to tell me what he knows and why they did it, and I really don't want you to see that."

"Ok" she said dejectedly.

"Don't be like that. You'll get credit for the collar, and I'll even let you arrest him."

"Thanks, Cap."

Her mood lightened a little but not much. She headed back to her desk to wait until he said she could come back to his office. A few minutes later she saw Jefferson walk by on his way to the captain's office. She avoided looking at him for fear he would be able to see the disgust on her face.

14

"You wanted to see me, Captain Layton?"

"Yes, Jefferson, come on in. Close the door too, please."

"Sure, what's up?" he asked as he sat down in the chair opposite from the captain.

"It's about this," Layton said as he threw the fingerprint card at Jefferson.

"Is there something wrong?"

"What's wrong is that these are your prints. They were found on the safe at Brad's house. You remember that scene, don't you? Home invasion, and Brad was in the hospital for over a month?"

"Yeah, I remember."

"So how did your fingerprints get on the safe in the closet in their bedroom?"

"I don't know. I don't even think we went in there to dust for prints."

"That's the problem. It was right there in the closet when you guys were up there, dusting for prints. This is the only thing that didn't have fingerprint powder on it. Can you tell me why that is?"

"I honestly can't tell you that. I don't know why it didn't."

"Is that a fact? No idea at all why you didn't dust this for prints, or didn't you dust it for prints because yours were already on it?"

"What are you getting at, Captain? Are you implying that I had something to do with this?"

"I certainly am! We can account for all the other prints on it except for yours and one other person's. You need to tell me who your partner is, and you need to tell me right now."

"What if I won't talk to you? What are you going to do then?"

"I'll have you arrested and put it squarely on your shoulders, and you'll go down for the crime, alone. When it comes time for sentencing, I'll suggest they throw the book at you for what you did to Brad. You and you alone will be accepting responsibility for all of it. How does that sound?"

"I didn't touch Brad. That was Ryan." Realizing what he just did, he hung his head and said, "I'll tell you everything."

"Just a minute, Jefferson." Layton called Sarah to come into his office.

"Hey, Cap, you called?" she asked, pretending not to know why.

"Yes, I'd like you to place Jefferson under arrest, read him his rights, and take his statement. Get this scumbag out of my office before I say something I'm going to regret."

"Yes, sir. On your feet, Jefferson. Let's go to a little quieter place, shall we?"

She led him out of the Captain's office and into and interrogation room. She left him in there so she could go get Shane so he could watch from the observation room.

"Thanks for letting me watch, Sarah. This is going to help me out a great deal."

"No problem."

Back in the interrogation room, she read Neal his rights, gave him a pad of paper to write his statement, and told him to tell her what happened.

"Well, I overheard Brad talking to his wife one day on the phone about 'putting that money in the safe when I get home,' and it piqued my interest. I was talking to a buddy of mine, and he said, we should go to their house and rob them or steal the safe. We laughed it off at the time, but then my wife and son were killed in a car accident out in Los Angeles, and I thought, *What the hell do I have to lose?* We made a plan, and once we started, I knew we wouldn't stop. The only thing I hadn't planned on was how violent Ryan got when we found out that someone was in the house. When we went in and Brad was there, Ryan went nuts. He started hitting him and then tied him up and asked where the safe was. Brad said it was upstairs, so we went up there and tried to open it. When Brad couldn't tell us the combination, he shot him. I thought he killed him, and when we left, I checked to make sure he was still breathing, but that's all I did. I felt awful for what happened to Brad, and when the case came up, I made sure I was the one that answered the call. I didn't dust the safe because we had done such a number on it. I didn't think anyone would even think about it."

"Why didn't you wear gloves? No one would have ever caught you. Brad doesn't remember much about that day, so he wouldn't have been able to ID you."

"I honestly didn't think that we would actually do it, especially after we got in and Brad was there. Thankfully, we had ski masks on, or he would have known me. I did it out of desperation and grief. I never meant for anyone to get hurt."

"I'm sorry for what happened to your family, but that doesn't give you the right to attack an innocent man in his own home and try to steal from him."

"I know, and I'm sorry. I don't know what else to say."

"I do. You're under arrest for the brutal attack on Detective Brad Hastings. Give me Ryan's information, and I will see if the DA will go easy on you because you cooperated. Stand up and put your hands behind your back."

Once Neal was handcuffed, he was led to a cell.

15

Sarah took the information that Neal had given her and went over to Ryan's house with Shane. They went up to the front door and knocked. The door was opened by a woman, and Sarah asked her if Ryan was around.

"Yeah, just a minute." She turned around and yelled into the house, "Ryan, cops are here to see you."

"Shit," was all they heard before they heard a door slam.

"Shane, go around back," Sarah yelled.

Shane ran around the back to see if he could stop Ryan. Thankfully, he was in the garage, waiting for the garage door to go up when Shane drew his weapon and told him to freeze. Sarah went running back and saw that Ryan was caught.

"Ryan James? You're under arrest for assaulting an officer with intent to kill."

She read him his rights as she put handcuffs on him. They led him back to the squad, brought him to the station, and put him in an interrogation room. Once he had given his statement, they put him in a cell. Sarah called Brad and told him the news.

"Are you serious? He was a CSI?"

"Yes, one was a CSI, Neal Jefferson, and a friend of his. We just arrested the friend. This should be all settled before you come back to work. I mean, there will be the trial unless they settle, but hopefully, you can put it all behind you and know that you and Mom are safe from them ever coming back to get what they didn't the first time."

"I can't believe it was Neal. I've worked with him in the past. This news will make your mother very happy."

"What about you? Are you happy?"

"Oh, I am, Sarah. It's just that I can't believe one of our own could do something like this."

"I know. I feel the same way. I think of this place as my second home, my second family, and then something like this happens. But, hey, we caught them, and they are going to pay for what they did, and that is something I'm very grateful for."

"You're right. I'm very happy you have such a good eye for details. Even after hearing the details, I'm still foggy on what happened. It's ok, though. If I never remember that night, it will be too soon. Thank you, Sarah, for letting me know and for figuring it out. See, you're going to make a wonderful detective."

"Thanks, Brad. That means a lot coming from you."

She went in to tell the Captain that Ryan had been arrested as well, and that should wrap up the case.

"Nice work, Sarah. You're first case as detective, and you solved it basically by yourself. That's pretty impressive, young lady."

"Thanks, Cap. That means a lot. I did let Brad know, too, that hopefully this will all be wrapped up except for the trial."

"They may settle, too, just because he worked for the police station."

"I sure hope so. I really don't want Mom and Brad to have to sit through another trial."

"I agree. We'll have to wait to see what the DA comes up with for them. Good thing Brad survived, or this could be a whole different ball game."

"Absolutely. On a different note, I'm working on a cold kidnapping case and was wondering if you would let me go out to Hollywood to interview Allan Larson?"

"Remind me who he is."

"He's the father of Jesse, the six-year-old that went missing around seven or eight years ago. He has a big mansion in Hollywood, and Brad said that since he is out of our jurisdiction, you told him he had to drop the case."

"I see that worked. What do you have for me to convince me that I should let you go out there to interview him again?"

"I don't have anything concrete. I really just want to get a feel for the guy. I have a feeling he might know more than what he lets on. I've read through the file and think it would help me out to interview him and see if he tells me more than he ever told Brad. Maybe because I'm a woman, he'll open up a little bit about it."

"I don't know if I want you to go out there on a 'feeling'. I really need to see something that would give you reason to go out there. If you can show me that, I'll let you go. I know you have an eye for detail, so bring me something."

"Ok, I'll keep looking."

She walked out of his office, sat back down at her desk, and started to go over that file one more time. Sarah was about half way through the file when Nate came up to see if she was ready to go home.

She looked at him and said, "Uh, yeah, I'm ready. I just need to take this one home with me. How did your day go?" she asked him as she locked up her desk.

"It was busy. How about yours?"

"Great. We arrested the two guys that were involved in the home invasion at Brad and Mom's."

"You did? Oh, honey, that's terrific. This calls for a celebration," he exclaimed excitedly.

"I'd really just rather go home and look through this file. We can celebrate later this week. Maybe we'll have more to celebrate."

"What could be this exciting?"

"I could solve this old kidnapping case."

"I'm sure you're going to give it your best shot."

"You know it. Are you coming over to my place for dinner?"

"I thought you wanted to work on this file?"

"I do, but I still have to eat."

"Well, if you're inviting me over, then yes, I'd like to come over for dinner. What are we making?"

"I'll stop at the grocery store and pick up something. What are you in the mood for?"

"How about this: I'll stop at the store. You go home and get started on the file. When I get there, I'll make dinner while you work."

"You really want to do that?"

"If it means spending more time with you, then yes, I really want to do that."

"You are incredibly sweet."

She finished getting everything together to bring home with her and gave Nate a quick kiss. They walked out to the parking lot, where she drove him home, said goodbye, and they went in separate directions.

16

WHEN SARAH GOT home, she changed into comfy clothes and sat on the sofa, reading through the rest of the file, waiting for Nate to come over. She let him up when he buzzed, and he went right to work in the kitchen. Sarah turned the final page over and felt incredibly sad for this poor girl. She wanted to reach out to Shelly and give her a big hug and tell her everything was going to be ok. There weren't a lot of crime-scene photos, only pictures of the parking lot and surrounding cars. Sarah was taking notes as she went through the file, and she added security cameras to it since she didn't see anything about it in the file.

She got up, walked into the kitchen, put her arms around Nate's waist, and said, "Something sure smells good."

"Hey, no fair, distracting the cook." He laughed. "It's my specialty, garlic butter steak with home fries and grilled asparagus."

"It looks as good as it smells," she said as she moved to stand next to him.

"It does, doesn't it? How are you doing on your case?"

"I'm finished reading through it, but now I need to make more notes on what I think is missing. I didn't see in the report that they looked at any security-camera footage from the grocery store. Maybe they never thought about it, or maybe they didn't have any. That's the kind of stuff I'm looking for. I want to talk to my mom about the father's house in Hollywood. I want to know what kind, if any, of hiding spots there may be in an old house like that. It's a huge old house that may have had slaves at one time, and at the time this happened, they had servants. I need to know if a house that old would have any secret rooms, like the one I was put in when I was kidnapped."

"What makes you think that your mom would know?"

"She might not know, but maybe she can point me in the right direction on who to ask about it."

"Ah, that makes sense. Do you want to throw some things at me and see if I can help?"

"Maybe after dinner. I've had enough of work for now. Are we almost ready to eat?"

"Yeah, it should be ready in about five minutes. Do you want to eat at the table or in the living room?"

"I'll set the table, and then we can eat in here."

"Sounds like a great idea."

He turned away from the stove, reached out to her, and pulled her to him. He kissed her and wrapped his arms around her like he never wanted to let go. She leaned against him and sighed, a happy, content sigh.

"I sure do like this," he said.

"Mmhmm, me too." She moved away and set the table. Once she was done, Nate dished up their plates.

"Holy cow, that's a lot of food," she exclaimed.

"I want you to keep your strength up. Can't have you wasting away to nothing, now, can I?"

"You don't have to worry about that. I eat plenty." She cut her steak and took a bite, and it melted in her mouth. "Wow, this is fantastically delicious, melt-in-your-mouth goodness. Where did you learn to cook?"

"I learned from my mom. Dad used to like to have lavish parties, and Mom was the one stuck cooking everything. When I was old enough, I helped her. I've got a lot of great recipes up my sleeve."

"I can't wait! How are your mom and dad? You don't talk about them much."

"My parents are both deceased. They were killed in a skiing accident in Aspen about three years ago."

"Oh, honey, I'm so sorry."

"It's ok. Sometimes it's hard, like when we got engaged, I didn't have anyone to call and share my news with, but for the most part, it's good."

"You don't have brothers or sisters?"

"No. I, like you, was an only child."

"How did I not already know this about you?"

"Because I don't talk about myself very much. We've always had something way more interesting going on than talking about me."

"I hope those exciting days are behind us now. I don't want that kind of excitement in my life if it means potential harm to me or ones that love."

"I totally understand. How's the rest of your meal? Satisfactory?"

"Way more than satisfactory. I haven't had a steak this good ever, I don't think."

"Well, thank you. I'm glad you are enjoying it. My mom taught me well."

"She certainly did. Want to watch a movie after we clean up?"

"Sure, that sounds nice and relaxing."

They finished eating, cleaned up the kitchen, and went to go see what movie they wanted to watch.

"Comedy, drama, or chick flick?" she asked.

"Comedy all the way, baby."

"Ok, sounds good to me too."

She flipped through some channels, found a movie they both wanted to watch, and then curled up with Nate on the couch. As they watched the movie, her eyes kept getting heavier and heavier. Pretty soon Nate could hear her snoring softly. *Poor thing*, he thought, *she's been running herself ragged. I should get out of here and let her sleep. I'll just put her to bed.* He picked her up, carried her to her room, changed her clothes, and tucked her in. He gave her a kiss on the forehead and let himself out. He drove back to his house and realized for the hundredth time how much he loved being with her and how much he wanted to go back and stay with her. *Until she decides if she wants to move in together, I'll take what she gives me.* He finished watching the movie they had started at her house, got ready for bed, and turned in early.

Around 2:00 a.m. Sarah woke up in bed and was a little confused. *How did I get here? The last thing I remember is watching a movie with Nate.* She looked next to her, no Nate. *He must have put me to bed, and what, left? Or is he sleeping on the couch?* She got up, went to the living room to see if Nate was there, but again, no Nate. She went to the door and put the chain on, went to the bathroom, got a drink of water, and went back to bed. She thought about calling him, but it was awfully late, so she decided not to. As she laid there, she thought about something from the cold case and had to get up and write it down. *One more thing to ask when I talk to Mom,* she thought. She drifted back to sleep within moments of laying back down.

17

THE ALARM WENT off at 6:00 a.m., and Sarah felt refreshed and ready for the day. *That was the best night's sleep I've gotten in a long time*, she thought. She texted Nate a good morning, got in the shower, and got ready for her day. She called Captain Layton about 7:00 to tell him she was going to swing by the grocery store where Jesse had been kidnapped and then was going to stop at Brad's to get some more information from him. She pulled up to the store and noticed right away that there were cameras by the entrance and several of them scattered throughout the lot. *I wonder how long they've had these?* She went into the store, told them who she was, why she was there, and asked to speak to a manager.

The manager walked up to her and said, "Detective Wheeler? I'm Sam, the manager, what can I do for you?"

Sarah extended her hand and said, "It's a pleasure to meet you, Sam. Please call me Sarah. I'm here investigating a cold case about a little girl that was kidnapped out in the parking lot. Were you working here when it happened?"

"Oh, yes, I was, and it was one of the most awful days. That poor mom, Shelly, came running back in here, screaming her daughter's name, 'Jesse! Jesse, this isn't funny, come out here this instant.' That little girl was nowhere to be found. We searched the entire store—the parking lot and the dumpsters, everywhere we could think. It was so difficult to watch that poor mom and not being able to help her."

"How long have the cameras been outside?"

"Oh, I'd say we got them six to seven years ago. Why?"

"Do you know if it was before Jesse went missing?"

"We might have had the one in the store and above the door outside, but the ones in the parking lot have only been there for three years."

"Did anyone watch the footage from inside the store to see if Jesse had come back in or to see if someone had followed them out to the car?"

"I don't recall anyone looking at the tapes from back then. Do you think there might have been something on it?"

"There might be. Especially the one by the door. Maybe the kidnapper was in the store and took advantage of a situation. I don't suppose you still have the tape or footage from that day, do you?"

"I'm not sure. I'd have to get in touch with the home office. All of our footage is streamed right there, and they keep it, but I'm not sure for how long."

Excitedly she asked, "Can you give me a phone number to contact someone in the home office? This could be just what we need to get this investigation kickstarted again."

"I most certainly will give you whatever you need to help. I'll be back in a jiffy."

When he returned, Sarah was in the same place she had been when he left. He handed her a business card and had handwritten a name for their IT person.

"You have been most helpful, Sam. Thank you so very much."

"I would do whatever I could to help out that family. That poor mother. I'm a father. I don't know how she has gotten through the last how many years, not knowing if her daughter is dead or alive."

"If you think of anything else at all, please don't hesitate to call me." She handed him her card with her cell and station numbers on it. "Again, Sam, thank you for helping me with this."

"You are more than welcome. I just hope if she's alive still that you guys find her."

"So do I."

She walked back out to her car, called her mom to see if she was home, and headed over there to talk to her about an old mansion.

18

SHE PULLED INTO the driveway, walked up to the door, and knocked. Her mom came to the door and let her in.

"Hello, sweetheart, what brings you by?"

"I need to talk to you about an old mansion in Hollywood. I'd like to talk to Brad about that cold case I'm working on too. Is he here?"

"He is. Come on into the living room, and we'll try to help you out."

"Thanks, Mom."

They walked into the living room, and Lynda called out to Brad, "Hon, Sarah is here to talk about the cold case. Would you please come out here?"

"Sure, be right there." Brad came out from the kitchen with a couple of breakfast burritos. "Hungry, Sarah?"

"No, thanks."

"Ok, what can I do for you?"

"Well, I have some questions for both of you. First, Mom, what do you know about old mansions in Hollywood?"

"Honestly, honey, I don't know a great deal. What are you looking for?"

"I need to know if places like that had slave quarters or servant quarters or any secret rooms like a bomb shelter."

"Oh, like if they have separate entrances and such?"

"Yes, that's exactly what I need to know."

"I wouldn't be able to tell by looking at it, obviously, but if there are places like that in Hollywood, they might be registered with the county. You could find out if they have a copy of the blueprints on file. They should tell you if there are servants' entrances and passages throughout the house. Why do you ask?"

"It's this kidnapping case. I thought about what happened to me, and the only way they could keep me out of sight was to put me somewhere no one knows about. If Allan Larson had taken her, what better place to keep her than the servants' quarters? How many people would even know they were there except for the guy that owns the place? It just seems that she disappeared without a trace, just like I did, but someone knows where she is. There's never been a body found. What do you think, Brad? Am I off my rocker?"

"Actually, that is a very good idea. I don't think that we ever thought about something like that."

"I have something else too. I went back to that market and asked about their security cameras, and he said he wasn't sure if anyone ever viewed their footage inside or by the door of the store. Do you know if anyone ever looked at it?"

"I'm not sure if we did or even thought about it back then. It should be in the report if we did."

"I didn't see anything in there about it, but I wanted to check with you first."

"These are both great new ideas, Sarah. Have you talked to Layton about going to Hollywood?"

"I did, and he said only if I had something solid to go on could I go and talk to Allan. Do you think I have enough to pay him a visit?"

"I'd see if you could find blueprints on the house to see if they in fact have any hidden rooms or corridors before I bring it to the captain."

"Ok, I'm going to go back to the office and call the county and see if they can help me. Thanks, you guys, you've been a big help."

"Anytime, dear," her mom said as she walked with her to the door and waved as she walked to her car. "What do you think of that, Brad?"

"I think she's going to be a terrific detective, and I'm damn glad that she's my partner. This makes me want to go back to work even more now."

"What about going in and helping out at the station? I bet they could use your help with phone calls and whatnot."

"I hate making calls, but it would get me used to being there again, and I wouldn't have to stay all day. I think I'll call Layton and see what he thinks."

"Oh, that sounds wonderful. I think I'll call my boss and tell him I'm ready to come back to work too. Once you go back full-time, I'll go back full-time too. Shouldn't be too many more years, and we can retire and not have to worry about it."

"That will be a very happy day. Wanna fool around?"

"Brad! Right now? I thought you were going to call the captain?"

"I can call him after."

19

ARMED WITH THIS new information, Sarah went back to the station to call the Los Angeles county clerk's office to see if they could help with those blueprints. She was told that the person that normally handled that was out sick today. Damn. She was really hoping that she would've gotten that information today to bring it to the captain so she could go talk to this guy, Allan. She tried the home office of the grocery store and was told that they needed to look into it and would call her back.

When she told them she needed it as soon as possible, they said they'd look today and call her back. She left her cell phone number and thought, *I can't get anything done today with this case*. All of a sudden there was a commotion; cops were running toward the front of the building, and Sarah wondered what was happening. She followed everyone else to see what was going on.

From where she was, she couldn't see anything, but she could hear yelling and then a gunshot. It's like time stood still. Most of the other officers drew their weapons, unsure of who shot or who got shot. She couldn't believe this was happening at the station. What the hell is going on? She went back toward the interior of the station and saw that the captain was in his office on the phone. She could hear him yelling from where she was. As she got closer to his office, he motioned her in.

He hung up abruptly and asked angrily, "What in Sam Hill is going on out there?"

"I don't know. I heard yelling and a shot. I retreated 'cause I couldn't see anything."

"Well, shit. I need to know if one of our guys is down or what is going on." They started to see more officers coming back into the station. Layton yelled at one of them, "What's going on out there?"

"There was a kid out there, high on something, and he was waving a gun around and tried to get inside. He was stopped, and when he was, he shot at one of our guys but missed and was tackled. He's on his way to the hospital to check for injuries and to see if we can determine what kind of drugs he's on."

"So it's all taken care of?" the captain asked.

"Yes, sir, all the excitement is over."

"Thank God for small miracles." Sarah returned to her desk and saw Nate coming toward her.

"Are you ok?" he asked her.

"Yes, I'm fine, why?"

"I just heard about the gunshot but no one knew if anyone was hit. I'm glad it wasn't you."

"No, I was too far in the back to even get to see what happened. According to Smitty, the guy with the gun was high on something, and when he fired, he missed and is on his way to the hospital to see if he's ok and if they can determine what kind of drugs he's on."

"That's crazy that this would happen here. I'm just glad you're ok."

"I'm fine. You don't have to worry about me so much, you know."

"I know, but I still do. Are you free for lunch?"

"Yes, I've been hitting brick wall after brick wall today, so anytime you want to get out of here, let me know."

"Let's go now. I'll go down and lock everything up at my desk and be right back up."

When Nate left, Sarah grabbed a couple more cold-case files and locked up her desk.

"All set?" Nate asked.

"Sure am. I don't think that I'll come back today either. I'm going to go home and read these two other files to see if I can catch anything that may have been missed. Oh, by the way, thank you for putting me to bed last night. I'm so sorry for falling asleep on you."

"It's not a big deal. You've been working hard, and I was more than happy to let you sleep."

"It was incredibly sweet of you, and I was a little shocked that I was in bed all tucked in when I woke up."

"Again, it was no problem. Where do you want to go eat? Oh wait, let me guess, pizza?"

"Ha, not this time, smarty-pants. I want to go and have a nice, juicy burger."

"Will you never cease to amaze me?"

"Oh, probably someday, but I'm hoping that is a long time down the road."

"You are something else, Sarah Wheeler."

"Oh? And what is that something else?"

"You are the love I've been looking for, the woman of my dreams, my princess—"

"Oh, stop it, you," she said, laughing.

"What's the matter? Can't handle all that mushy talk?" he asked with a grin on his face.

"Oh, I can handle it. It's just getting a little deep in here, is all."

"Ah, c'mon Sarah. How can you say such things to me? I'm mortally wounded from your harsh words." He tried to sound pathetic as he said this but failed miserably when he started to laugh at her expression.

"Wow, will you stop at nothing for sympathy?"

"Nope, not if it means that I'll get a hug from you. You know, so you can heal my mortally wounded soul."

"You are one funny man, aren't you, Nathan? Well, mister, let's go to Slyderz Grill, and we can talk about your mortally wounded whatever."

"Cool, I may need examining later too."

"Oh, will I need to bring you to the doctor?"

"Well, I was hoping that you would examine me."

"Were you, now? Well, we'll have to see. I'm not going back to the station today, but I will be working from home. How about you?"

"I think I can take the rest of the day off. But if you're going home to work, I might as well go back to work. I won't get any of your attention." he said, pouting.

"Aw, poor baby, look at that lip sticking out. That is so sad. I bet I could sneak in a couple minutes for you."

"Oh boy, oh boy, oh boy," he said, pretending to be excited. "A whole couple of minutes? How will I ever contain myself?"

"All right, how about this, if you want to take the rest of the day off, you and I can examine your soul and have dinner, but after that, I really want to read through at least one of these files."

"All work and no play…"

"Let's just go eat," she said exasperatedly but with a grin.

20

ONCE THEY FINISHED with lunch, Nate drove them to his place instead of Sarah's. He lived in a nice small house in a quiet neighborhood.

"We hardly ever come here, and since we're engaged, I thought maybe you'd like to see what it's like around here. It's quiet but nice. The house may be small, but it's enough for right now. If we decide to have kids, then we'd need a bigger place unless you just want to buy a new house together. I'm in for whatever you decide."

"I do like your place. It is a little small for kids, but we could make it work if we had to."

They went inside and decided to do a little of their own fooling around. They were cuddling in bed with Nate stroking her arm and Sarah's head on his chest. Her cell phone went off, and she grabbed it to see who was calling. It wasn't a number she recognized but answered it since she was waiting for calls on her cold case.

"Hello, this is Detective Wheeler."

"Hi, this is the Nikki from the Los Angeles county clerk's office. I understand that you are looking for some information on one of the houses in Hollywood. Is that right?"

"Yes, thanks for calling me back. Can you tell me if you have blueprints for this address—3737 Lancaster Boulevard, Hollywood?"

"Let me take a look. Do you have a minute or two for me to check it out, or would you like me to call you back?"

"I can wait. It's very important for me to get this information as soon as possible. It concerns a kidnapped little girl, and I need to see those prints."

"Ok, please hold, and I'll be right back with you."

"Thank you." Sarah was placed on hold and, putting her hand over the receiver, told Nate, "It's going to be a few minutes, but I should know today if they have them. This is very good news!"

"I'm glad they got back to you so quickly," he said. He got up, put some clothes on, and went to the kitchen. When he came back with bottles of water for them, she was still on hold. "Here you go, babe."

"Thanks, you're so considerate."

"Hello? Detective Wheeler?"

"Yes, I'm here."

"We do have copies of those blueprints. Do you want to stop and pick them up?"

"Is there any way that you can e-mail them to me?"

"I don't think so. They are rather large. The house is over ten thousand square feet."

"I guess I'll have to come and pick them up then. I won't be able to come and get them until tomorrow, though."

"Let me see if I can break it down enough to send in an e-mail."

"You can send it in as many e-mails as it takes you. I'm fine with that."

"Ok, let me see what I can do. If you don't see something from me in the next couple of minutes, call me back, and maybe we can get something else to work." Sarah gave her e-mail address to Nikki, who gave Sarah her direct line to call back. Once they hung up, Sarah grabbed her tablet to wait for the e-mail.

"I sure hope she can get these to me today. I need to see if they have any kind of slave/servants' quarters listed. If everyone thinks it was the father of this little girl, but no one has found a body or seen her at his house, this would be the way to see if he is keeping her. We could go in armed with this knowledge, and it would be included on the search warrant."

"Why don't you come back over here and snuggle with me some more?"

"Oh, Nate, I would, but I really need to watch for these." When she saw how disappointed he was, she said, "Oh ok, I can snuggle and wait at the same time." She laid back down with her head on his chest, and they just laid there, holding each other.

"This is nice," Nate said.

"Yes, it is. I could get used to this."

"You could if we lived together, but when it doesn't happen very often, it's hard to get used to."

"I know. We've only been engaged for a few days. Give me some time to get used to it, and we'll talk about it again soon. I promise."

"Oh, all right. I guess I can give you a couple weeks." He winked at her when she looked up at him. "I'm sorry, Sarah. I just want to spend as much time with you as I can. I miss you when you aren't with me. I love spending time with you, and I just want to know that you are safe."

"I know, Nate, and maybe if we spend a couple of nights with each other, it will tell me if I'm ready to move in with you. If I don't think I'm ready then, I really think we should wait a little longer. Can we do a 'practice run' at this? What if we get on each other's nerves so bad we want to kill each other, then what? I really would like to take this slowly. I want us both to be sure that this is what we both want."

"I understand. I don't think that I could ever be mad enough at you to want to kill you, but you never know. I'm kind of feeling like that right now." He smirked at her when she looked up at him. "I'm only kidding. But seriously, I'll give you the time you need even if I don't like it."

"Thank you for that, Nate. You are, after all, my first real boy-friend since I was fifteen."

"I still find that so hard to believe. I would have thought you would have been snapped up at the drop of a hat."

"I wasn't allowing myself to get snapped up. Until I met you and you showed genuine care and concern for me, I didn't give a rip if I ever had another boyfriend."

"Well, then I'm glad that the captain sent me to your house instead of someone else. From the moment I met you, I wanted to go out with you."

"That was obvious. You asked me out within hours of meeting me." Her tablet went off, alerting her to an e-mail. She reached for it, and it was an e-mail from the county clerk's office. Then there was another and another.

"Here come some e-mails from the clerk's office. I should probably go home so that I can get some work done."

"I thought we were going to have dinner?"

"How about this: how about we go back and get my car, stop for something for dinner, and you can spend the night at my place?"

"I like the sound of that. Let me grab some stuff to bring over to your house so I don't have to come back here in the morning."

"Ok, I'll get dressed and ready to go."

After about fifteen minutes, they were ready to go.

21

NATE HAD TOLD her to go on home and that he'd meet her there after he grabbed dinner. When he buzzed her apartment around 5:30, Sarah was engrossed in the blueprints from Allan Larson's house. She buzzed him up and unlocked the door when she could see him. He had two big bags with him.

"What's all this? How many people are we feeding for dinner?"

"I got extra just in case we need a snack for later." They went into the kitchen to dish up dinner and went in the living room to eat. "So how's it going, looking over those blueprints?"

"It's long and tedious. I really don't know what I'm looking for but thought if anything looked odd, I'd figure it out, but I may not be the best person to find what I'm looking for. It doesn't help that they are only the size of my tablet screen. If I looked at them on my computer at the station, they would be a lot bigger."

"After dinner let me take a look. I've got an eye for detail." He had stopped and picked up Indian food at Guzzetti's, and they were digging in.

"Ok, you're on. Can you maybe help me figure them out a little bit?"

"I can try. I'm not sure if I will see anything, but if I do, I will certainly show you what I see."

They started eating, and Sarah raved at how good everything was, "I've got to admit, I've never eaten Indian food before. It is really good. I'm pleasantly surprised."

"You've never had Indian food?" he asked incredulously. "It's one of my favorite cuisines."

"See, that's something we didn't know about each other ten minutes ago. I'm always afraid to try new stuff. What if I don't like it? I'm stuck with food I won't eat, and I'm still hungry. At least with pizza, I know I'll eat it."

"You need to branch out a little bit, honey. There's a whole lot of food out there just waiting for you to try."

"I really like whatever it is you picked out, but you might not want to tell me what it is just yet. If it's anything other than chicken or beef, I'm not sure that I could handle that right now," she said with a laugh.

"Ok, note to self: do not tell Sarah what we eat."

"What? Ok, what are we eating? Now I'm scared and don't want to eat any more of it," she said with a sad face.

"It's ok, it's lamb. You've had a gyro before, right?"

"Um, well, not really."

"What do you mean, not really? Did you taste it and not eat it, or did you think about it and decide that since it was lamb, you wouldn't eat it?"

"I'd say that I was going to try it and then found out it was lamb and wouldn't eat it. But I'd eat it now if this is what it tastes like. This is very good."

"Oh boy, you're going to have an entire world of food open up to you. This is going to be fun," he said as he watched her sample some of the other things he put out. "You have to try it all too. No one is here to judge you if you don't like something, and I like it all, so what you don't eat means more for me."

"I'm trying it all. I'm just not sure how I feel about all of it. Some of it smells a little weird."

"It's because they use way different spices than we do around here." They continued to eat and chat, and when they finished cleaning up, Nate said, "Ok, show me those prints, and I'll take a look at them to see if I can see anything."

"Oh, thank you. I appreciate you helping me out."

"No problem. I like being here with you, and even if we're working, at least we're together."

She smiled at him as she pulled up the blueprints and handed him her tablet. As he was looking through them, she was half-looking along with him and half-relaxing after dinner.

"This might be something. Look at this."

"What? I don't see anything."

"Here," he said, pointing to a shaded portion of the plan that looked like it could be under the kitchen of the current house.

"It doesn't look like anything but a shadow."

"I know, but it could mean that there is a corridor or something under the kitchen. Let's look at some of the other rooms to see if we see more shading."

"You really think so? Ok, let's look." They changed pages and saw a few more spots where there was shading under a room of the main floor of the house.

"Do you know if this place has a basement? I don't see any plans for a lower level."

"I don't know if it does or not. I thought she sent me all pages, but maybe not. It's past quitting time for them, so I'll have to reach out to her tomorrow, but that's a good thing to ask. I'll ask her about the shaded areas too. Thanks, sweetie, for helping me. I wouldn't have thought that was anything at all."

"It might not be, but it seems to be in certain areas too, not the size of the whole main level. That would mean that if these were corridors or rooms under the main level, there isn't a lot of space down here. We also need to see if we can find a flight of stairs or way that they would get up to the main level or if this is strictly cut off from the rest of the house. Once you talk to her tomorrow, we can be more sure of what we're looking at."

"Wow, this is turning out to be more of a task than I thought. I was hoping it would be like a flashing neon sign pointing to it, saying, 'Here is the underground stuff you were looking for,' but I see that is not going to be the case. Well, I'm ok with hanging this up for today and, after talking to Nikki tomorrow, working on it again. See, aren't you glad you came over? We're done with the blueprints and dinner. Whatever will we do for the rest of the evening?"

"I thought you wanted to read over one of these other cases?"

"Since I got the blueprints, I'd actually like to just work on this one for now."

"Well, in that case, I have an idea on what we could do for the rest of the evening."

"Oh? I'm curious as to what that might be?"

He took her by the hand and led her to her bedroom where he showed her what they could do for the rest of the evening.

22

BEFORE GOING TO the station in the morning, Sarah stopped at her mom's to see if either she or Brad knew how to read blueprints. She walked up to the door, knocked, and was told to come in. She walked in to see that they were just sitting down to breakfast.

"Good morning, dear. Care to join us for some breakfast?"

"Nah, I had breakfast with Nate."

Lynda's eyebrows went up, and she couldn't help but ask, "Did you make breakfast, or did you guys go out?"

"He made breakfast. Yes, mom, you don't even have to ask. He stayed overnight. We've been talking about moving in together since we are engaged, but I haven't decided if I want to do that just yet."

"Oh honey, I think it's a fine idea to move in together. He'd be there to protect my little girl. I know, I know, "you're a cop, you can protect yourself." I worry about you. It's my job as a parent to do that. If you moved in with Nate, I wouldn't worry as much. You'd also know if you could stand living with someone for the rest of your life. Call it a trial run, but I think it's a good idea."

"Well, his house is awfully small. If we plan on having kids, it won't be big enough for us and children. Anyway, the reason I stopped by is to see if either of you know how to read blueprints."

"Well, I don't know a ton about them, but I could look at them and see if I can pick up on something."

"What about you, Brad, do you know how?"

"Not really, I'm kind of in the same boat as your mom. I could look them over and see, but I'm probably not the one that could help you."

"Where could I go to show these to someone? I have them on my computer but would like to have them printed. Maybe they will be easier to read."

"Talk to Layton. He may know someone that can help you. You might have to even take them to a place that can print something that big to get them so you can read them."

"Ok, it was worth a shot coming here. Have a great day, guys. See you soon."

With a little bit more information, Sarah headed to the station. Once she got there, she went to the captain's office to see if he knew of anyone that could help. He told her to check with the county clerk's office; they would be able to help her out. She called the clerk's office to see when she could see someone that might be able to help. They told her to come down whenever she wanted to. She headed back out the door in hopes that someone would be able to help her figure this out.

When she arrived at the county clerk's office, she explained what she needed help with and was told to have a seat and someone would be with her shortly. While she waited, she pulled out her tablet and fired it up, ready to show the blueprints to whoever was going to help her. A young man come out and asked if she had come looking for help reading the prints. When she said yes, he asked where they were, and she told him on her tablet. He told her that they would need to be printed and to please follow him.

They went into his office, and he told her, "Hi. By the way, my name is Steve. Send those prints to me, and I can print them out, and then we can have a look at them."

"Nice to meet you. I'm Detective Wheeler."

She e-mailed the prints to him, and he printed them out. After he gathered them up, he returned to his office and laid them out on a plotters table.

"Ok, let's look at what we've got. What are you hoping these will tell you? Since you're with the police, I'm guessing you're hoping that these have some sort of information in them."

"Yes, I'm hoping they will tell me if there are any hidden exits/entrances or corridors. This is an old house, and the man that lives there is under investigation in the disappearance of his daughter. If I could find out if this house has hidden passages and such, I might be able to go out there and search his house to try to find this little girl."

"Wow, this is kind of exciting. We don't get much of this around here. Let's see what we've got." He looked them over, making comments to himself, jotting some stuff down, and when he was finished, looked at Sarah and smiled and said, "Well, from what I can see, it looks like there is definitely a separate entrance for servants. It is clearly marked on the blueprint, though, so I'm guessing you're looking for something that isn't so obvious. I did find this" he said and pointed to the shaded area under the kitchen. "Normally, there is nothing shaded as you can see from the rest of the prints. Since this is shaded, it leads me to believe that there may be a corridor or room under the kitchen. I see a few other spots like this, but it's not consistent with the rest of the prints. I would say that there is a very good chance that they have servants' room and such in the subbasement even though such a thing doesn't show up on their prints."

"Do you think you can show me how to get in there?"

"Well, let's see. Hmm, I see some hidden break and phantom lines that could mean nothing but could mean that exactly what you're looking for is under the kitchen and dining rooms. Now, the upstairs shows the dimensions of said rooms. If you go under these rooms, the lines are light and dotted, so it might show the exact location for the hidden room or rooms and how large they may be. Is this making any sense at all?"

"It is a little bit. What I need to know is how we get in to search this hidden area."

"Like I said before, I see a servant's entrance, and it may have a set of stairs that go down as well as up to the kitchen. They were very clever when they added these to the prints. They are very faint and hard to detect, but with what I see here, you should be able to use the servant's entrance to access the hidden areas under the kitchen and dining room."

"Wow, this is hard to believe. I can't thank you enough for showing me all of this. May I take these with me?"

"Absolutely. Anything to help the police find a missing child. I wish you the best of luck in finding her."

"Thank you again. You've been most helpful."

She couldn't believe it; she might actually find this little girl, if she was still alive. She prayed that she was. She headed right to the captain's office when she returned.

23

"Hey, Cap, got a second?"

"Ah, yeah, Wheeler, come on in. What's up?"

"Well, as you know, I'm working that cold kidnapping case. I have some new information that I'm hoping will get me into his house to see if I can find her."

"Oh? What have you got to show me?"

"Well, I was at the county clerk's office today to see if they could help me read the blueprints of Allan's house, and he was able to show me some things. Do you want me to show you too or just tell you?"

"Better show me in case the commissioner has questions about why I let you go looking in this guy's house after so many years."

She laid them out on his desk and showed him what Steve had shown her.

"So Cap, can I get a search warrant based on this new information? Even if he's not right, I would get a chance to talk to this guy for myself and see how he acts. My gut tells me he's up to something though."

"If it were up to me, Wheeler, I'd sign off on a search warrant so you could go and check it out. It's up to the judge to ok a search warrant."

"Which judge can we use? Is there one that would be more likely to sign off on it than another? Do they believe in gut instincts? Can I go talk to one of them today and try to get this signed?"

"Sarah, slow down a little bit. We have to make sure we have all components so they will sign off on it. Why don't you go get started on it, and I'll see who's in chambers today?"

"I'll get on it right now. I want to get out there tomorrow morning and get this search started. Any chance that I can take a few other cops with me? I don't want to go it alone you know just in case he is hiding his child there. I don't want him to try to harm her or me."

"Let's see what the judge has to say, and then we'll see what our next step is going to be."

She went to her desk to write up her warrant. She was almost finished when Layton called her desk phone and told her that they were in luck. Judge Bartleson was in chambers today, and that was a good sign.

"Great, do you want me to bring this in for you to look over?"

"No, if you have the information that we need to get it signed, bring it over to the judge."

"I'm on my way."

She finished up the little bit she had left on it and went to go see the judge. She got to his office and told his secretary, Angie, that she was there to get a signature on a warrant.

"Do you have an appointment?"

"No. Captain Layton told me come over here and get it signed."

"Since the captain told you to come up, I'll call him for you. Go ahead and have a seat, I'll let you know when he can see you."

"Thank you."

24

SHE SAT IN the waiting room for about fifteen minutes when she was told she could go to his office.

When she walked into his office, she said, "Judge Bartleson? I'm Detective Sarah Wheeler, and I'm here to see if you will sign my search warrant on a cold case to see if I can find a missing girl."

"Good to meet you, Detective. Have a seat and let me look it over." She handed him the warrant. As he read, he asked a few questions, and when he was done, he signed the warrant. "I sure hope you can find her. Good luck."

"Thank you, Judge, very much. I hope I can find her too."

She left elated that she was going to get her shot at this guy. She walked back to the station and into Layton's office and showed him the signed warrant.

"Congratulations! Now, when do you want to go?"

"I want to leave today, stay overnight, and go see him before he might leave for work."

"That sounds like a good idea. I'll contact the local PD out there and have them meet you at his house at about 7:00AM. I sure hope that you find something. I know the local PD watches him to see if he is going to make any mistakes, but so far, nothing."

"I hope I find her. I'd love to put this guy behind bars for a very long time."

"Get out of here, Wheeler. Oh, Sarah?"

"Yeah, Cap?"

"Good luck. I hope you nail this bastard to the wall."

Sarah walked out with a smile on her face and a plan to get on the road as soon as possible. Before she left, she went in search of Nate to tell him what she was going to do, and of course, he didn't want her to go, but she told him she'd be fine, that the captain was going to have the local PD meet her out there, and it would be all good. She texted her mom next and then Brad, asking him if he wanted to tag along.

"You don't want me hanging around. This is your first big case to solve. You go and take the collar."

"I want you to come with. We're partners. You don't have to do anything. After all, you started this case, it's only fitting that you be there in case we find her and can wrap this up."

"Let me see what your mom thinks." She heard them talking, and when he came back on the line, he said, "Well, partner, looks like you're going to have a driving buddy. I'll be ready to go when you get here."

"Great! I'll go home, pack a bag, and come pick you up."

25

SHE PICKED UP Brad, who looked pretty excited, better than he had in weeks.

"You must really be looking forward to doing something other than sit in the house. You are positively aglow."

"I can honestly say two things: no one has ever told me I'm 'aglow', and I am super happy to be getting out of that damn house. It feels like the walls are dosing in on me."

"I totally understand," she said as she chuckled.

They chatted while she drove, and he commented, "I really like this car. I might have to get a new car, maybe not the exact same thing, but it rides and handles fantastically."

"Yeah, I love it. I'm glad that Mom talked me into getting it." They stopped for food after a couple of hours. While they were waiting for their food, Sarah asked, "Are you sure that you don't want to take the lead on this? It is your case."

"Absolutely not. You've done the work and found something that was missed. This is all you."

"I'm a little bit nervous. What if it's a bust?"

"Sometimes that happens, but Allan will know that we are still trying to find his daughter and that we haven't given up on her or on him as a suspect. If she is there, this is going to be talked about for years to come. A father that would kidnap his own daughter and put her in a place she can't ever leave? That's unheard of in my book. I can't wait to see the look on his face when we show up there tomorrow. I sure hope he's home."

"Me too. I couldn't really call and ask if he'd be there. I don't want to tip my hand. He might move her somewhere else, and then we'd never find her."

"You're doing it the right way, Sarah. Besides, my guy hasn't told me that he's been out of town or anything, so we should be ok in that respect, but I'll call him in a little bit here to make sure."

"I am really glad you decided to come with me. Having someone else to talk to about it makes it less intimidating. Any words of advice?"

"Listen to your gut. If it's telling you that little girl is in that house somewhere, then leave no stone unturned."

"My gut is telling me something isn't right in that house. Steve, the guy that looked at the blueprints yesterday said that whoever added the information to the prints did it in such a way that not many people would be able to spot it. He thinks that we should be able to use the servant's entrance to find our way down to the hidden area under the kitchen and dining room."

"In all of my years of experience, I have never had a case like this."

"I wouldn't have thought about hidden rooms if I hadn't been in one before. Who thinks to hide another human being? Why? Is he trying to get back at his wife? Is he just a freak and is torturing this poor girl? I just don't understand the why."

"You won't know the why until you ask him. That's if he has her."

"He's got to. Everything points to him."

"That's what I said when I worked this case. I just couldn't figure out where."

They drove for a little while in silence. Brad called his guy at the local PD in Hollywood to see if he noticed if Allan was out of town.

"Great, thanks, Dave, that's just what I wanted to hear."

"Let me guess, he's not out of town," Sarah asked.

"Right, he's in town and been spending a couple of days a week working from home. At least that's what Dave assumes he's doing. Wonder why?"

"Well, how old is Jesse by now if she's still alive, thirteen or fourteen? Maybe he's been spending more time with her because she's acting out and is tired of being there, hidden away. Maybe he lets her into the house while he's there but puts her back downstairs when he knows someone is coming over. I don't know. I just hope we can find her. Even if she's not alive, I'd still like to find her. It will give her mother some kind of closure, and she can move on. I still think about what happened to me every day. It's not something that you get over like that," she said and snapped her fingers.

"You really think about it that much? I'm sorry, Sarah, for what happened to you. I'm just glad we were able to put that family away for a little while."

"Me too. I do know that having that happen to me has made me a stronger, more-determined person to not let that sort of thing happen to me again. I'm more aware of what's going on. I don't do things without thinking about what could happen if it didn't go the way I planned. That's one of the reasons I never opened the door for that damn stalker. I wanted to but thought about it and knew if I opened that door, it would be a split second before he might have done something to me and taken me away."

"You are careful, I'll give you that. Just remember, if we ever get into a situation where it's your life or mine, save yourself. Don't play the hero. That's what will get you killed."

"Don't talk like that. Nothing is going to happen to us. You're going to retire, and you and Mom will be taking trips all over the place, and I'll still be slaving away, catching scum and putting them behind bars."

"Nothing *should* happen to us, but things go wrong, and all I'm saying is, if it looks like we might both die, save yourself."

"This kind of talk is depressing me. Can we change the subject please."

He chuckled and said, "Yes, of course. Sorry, just letting my partner know how I see things."

"Ok, I get it. It might not happen that way, but I get it."

26

THEY WERE ABOUT six hours into their seven-plus-hour drive when Brad's phone rang. Sarah could only hear his side of the conversation, so she had no idea what was going on.

Once he hung up, he said, "We're in luck. Dave said that Allan is home today. Do we want to do this tonight when we get there? We can get checked into the hotel and have the PD meet us out there tonight. There is no time listed on the warrant and when we can do this. It would come as a big surprise if we did this tonight."

"Hey, that's not a bad idea. Ok, let's do that. Will you make us reservations somewhere? I didn't think to do that before we left."

"Sure." Brad called around to a couple of hotels, trying to find one as close to Allan's house as possible. "All set. Two queen-sized rooms, about a half hour from Allan's house."

"Great. I'm starting to get nervous."

"Don't be, you'll be just fine. I'm going to call the PD there and see how many guys they can spare tonight. I'm going to make sure that my buddy, Dave, is there too. He's been watching this guy for years, and if it ends tonight, I want him to see it."

Brad called Dave back and invited him along for the search and then called the PD in Hollywood to see how many folks they could spare to execute a search warrant at this guy's house to try to find his daughter.

"Great news. They can give us half a dozen guys, plus you, Dave, and me. That should give us enough to get this done."

"I sure hope you're right. Are we going to meet them somewhere first so we can go over a plan of attack?"

"Yes, they'll meet us at the hotel, and we can go over everything there."

"Ok. I have the prints with me so I can show them what we are going to be looking for."

They arrived at the hotel, checked in, and brought their bags in. The other officers showed up, and they all went to Brad's room.

"Ok, listen up. Detective Wheeler is lead on this, so let's do what she says. She's going to explain what we're looking for and what to possibly expect. Go ahead, Sarah. Tell us what to do."

She got a little nervous, having all eyes on her, but knew that she needed to make them all understand the importance of this mission—to get that girl out of that house alive. She showed them the blueprints, explained what they were looking for, where they were going to look for it, and what the end results should be.

"Does anyone have any questions?"

"What if she isn't there?"

"If she isn't there, then at least we will know that for sure. I want to go in there and leave nothing to chance. This warrant is for the entire house. I want us looking in, under, and around everything there. Any other questions? Do you all understand what is needed from each of you?" Everyone nodded in agreement. "Good, let's roll."

Sarah took the lead on the way to Allan's house. Dave was riding with them, so he told her how to get there. No flashing lights or sirens were used; no point in letting him know they were on the way. Once they pulled up outside, everyone got out of their vehicles. They surrounded the house in case Allan tried to leave; he wouldn't be able to. Sarah, Brad, and Dave walked up to the front door. Sarah knocked and listened, trying to hear movement inside.

The door was pulled open, and a woman answered the door, "Yes, may I help you?"

"Yes, I'm Detective Wheeler from the Chico PD, and we have a search warrant to search the premises. Is Mr. Sharpe home?"

"Just a minute I'll go check."

She went to close the door, but Sarah said, "You're not going to close this door and warn him that we're here. If it's all the same to you, we'll come in and wait."

"If that's what you'd like to do, suit yourself."

The three of them walked in and stood in the foyer. Sarah took the chance to look around at this massive mansion. She thought, *It reminds me of* Gone with the Wind. It was grandiose and glamorous. Everything was shining and clean. It didn't even look like anyone lived there.

When the woman who answered the door returned, she said, "He will be in momentarily. He's asked that you wait in the library."

"We'd like to wait here if it's all the same to you."

"He would really like you to meet him in the library."

"I don't care what he wants. He's not running the show here. We are." The woman turned around and walked away, never saying another word. They waited for what seemed like hours, but in reality, it was only about ten minutes.

He was coming down the giant staircase, and when he saw them standing by the door, he said, "I thought I told Sharon to put you in the library."

"She tried, but we are in kind of a hurry to get going. Mr. Sharpe, we have a search warrant to search your entire premises. You will stay with Detective Hastings while we search your house."

"What exactly are you looking for?"

"Why, we're looking for your daughter. We have reason to believe that she is being held here against her will."

"Go ahead and look around. You won't find her here. How many times will the police harass me? I've got one that comes by every once in a while and watches the house. They don't think that I know they are there, but I see them. I've told you guys a hundred—no, probably a thousand—times, you won't find my daughter here."

"I'm hoping that you're wrong about that, sir. I have blueprints from your house, and they show something that the officers didn't know about this house before only because you didn't tell them. There are secret rooms and corridors here, underneath the kitchen and dining room. I have a feeling that we will find your daughter down there."

Sarah thought that she saw a chink in his armor before his face returned to its same scowl.

"Now, then, Mr. Sharpe. May I call you Allan? Allan, we will need you to show us where that entrance is on the outside of the house, and then you will be escorted by Detective Hastings back into the house where you will stay until we have completed our search. Do I make myself clear?"

"Why can't you just leave me alone? I haven't done—"

"I said, do I make myself clear? I'm not going to listen to you whine while precious time is wasting away."

"Yes, perfectly clear, but I don't know where the servant's entrance is from outside. As far as I know, it's been boarded up since before I moved in."

"Ok, then show us how to get to the servant's quarters from inside the house. If you cooperate, things will go a lot smoother for you in the end. If we have to locate the boarded-up entrance from the outside, it won't be boarded up for long. We are prepared to tear it down board by board."

"I don't know what you're talking about. My servants all have rooms in one wing of the house. I can show you where that is, but otherwise, I'm not sure what you're getting at."

"What I'm getting at, Mr. Sharpe, is that your daughter has been missing for over seven years. Do you ever call the police to check and see if they have any new leads? Did you ever offer any suggestions as to where she might be? Did you ever tell the police, when they were here all those years ago, that there is more to this house than meets the eye? Have you ever done one thing to help find your little girl? She was six when she went missing. Aren't you even curious as to what has been done to try to find her? No, you're not, and you know why? Because you've had her here, held captive for all of these years, never thinking how awful it is for her to never see her mom or friends again. Did you even care that no one else in her family was able to see her again? No, because you're a selfish, narcissistic man who is keeping her for only reasons you know. I will find her here, you can count on it, and if I don't, I will charge you for her murder. Now, Mr. Sharpe, why don't you show me how to get to the rooms under the kitchen?"

"I don't know what you're talking about. How dare you come in here and accuse me of such madness. I'll have my lawyer sue you and the whole police department."

"Ok, let's do things your way. If you hear sounds of destruction, it's us trying to find the hidden servant's entrance since you claim to not know where it's at. Please go with Detective Hastings."

27

Sarah went outside to the rear of the house where the rest of the officers were waiting.

"Well, it looks like we're going to have to do this the hard way. Let's look at the prints and see if we can determine where that door was. He said it's been boarded up since before he bought the house. If that's the case, how did he even know about it? Let's find it and get it opened up."

They started searching for anything that would make them think a door had once been there. They had pry bars and once in a while would pry off a piece of siding but wouldn't find anything underneath.

About a half hour after they started, Sarah heard a shout, "I think I found something."

She ran over to where the officer was and asked him to show her. He pried the piece of siding off all the way, and underneath it was brick.

"That doesn't look very promising."

"No, it doesn't, but none of the other pieces I've pulled off has had brick underneath them. Makes me think we might be onto something."

"Good thinking. Now, how to we break down the brick?"

"Sledgehammer. I've got one in my squad."

"Honestly? Why do you keep one in your squad?"

"You never know when you're going to need one. I'll be right back." He ran out to get it, came back, and offered it to Sarah. "Detective Wheeler, would you like the first swing?"

"Thanks, I think I do." She swung back and then forward, and when it connected, the fake facade broke out. "What the hell? It's not even real brick? This will make everything easier."

The rest of the officers were called over, and in no time, they had the wall down. Behind the wall was a set of stairs that led to a very dark corridor. Sarah led the way flashlight in hand with a trail of officers behind her. As she went down the stairs, she was spurred on by hopes of finding that little girl and bringing her back home. When she saw a light switch, she flipped it on. A whole line of bare bulbs lit up the corridor. There were several rooms down there, and all the doors were closed. They stopped at each door, and the ones that were locked they left for later, wanting to see what laid ahead of them. They found a bathroom, a junk/storage room, and a game room that were all unlocked.

"She's got to be in one of these locked rooms. Anyone know how to pick locks?"

"I have a crowbar. We don't need to pick locks," Dave said.

"Ok, I'm going to knock on all of them before we break in just so we don't scare her."

She knocked on several doors with no answers and no one in them when they broke into them. *She's got to be here*, Sarah thought, *she just has to be.* There were only three rooms left. The next door they knocked on sounded different.

She knocked again and looked at Dave and said, "Does that sound differently than the others to you?"

"Yes, it does, like it's heavier than the others or solid all the way through." There was no answer at this door either, and when they tried to open it, the crowbar wouldn't open it. "What the hell are we going to use now to get it open?"

"Still have that sledge outside. I can run up and get it," said the cop who owned the sledgehammer.

"Yeah, ok, let's give that a try." When he returned, she took a whack at the door, but it hardly dented. "What in the world is this door made out of, cement?" she asked.

No one answered since she wasn't really looking for an answer; she was looking for a way in.

She thought about it for a minute and said, "I've got an idea. Stand back."

The other officers moved back, and Sarah moved directly to the left of the door to take a stab at trying to break through the wall. She brought the sledge back and slammed it into the wall. Sheetrock, dust, and debris were flying back at them.

"Well, count my lucky stars. The walls aren't made of the same stuff the door is."

One of the other officers came up behind her and asked, "Want me to do it?"

"Let me take a couple more swings. I'm envisioning someone's head right in that spot."

She took a few more swings, made a hole in the wall, but it was still too small to see inside the room. She relinquished the sledge, and the other officers took turns whacking at the wall.

28

When the hole was big enough for a head, she poked her head in the room. It was pitch dark in there. She put her flashlight in her mouth, stuck her head back in the opening, and tried to see what was in there. Because the opening was still too small to put her arm in, they opened it up wider.

She went in again, arms, head, and whistled, "Holy shit, guys, get this wall down now!"

They worked feverishly to get the wall down, wondering what Sarah saw.

The wall was finally big enough for people to get through, and Sarah went first, followed by Dave. She found the light switch and flipped it on just as the last cop was getting in the room. The room was all done in pink—something a little girl would love. There were all sorts of stuffed animals and a TV, along with several closed doors but not much of anything else.

She went to the first door and tried to open it; it was locked. She motioned for the guy with the crowbar over, and he popped it open. It was a closet. Next door was also locked. He pried that one open too, and it was a bathroom. The last door—the one Sarah was putting all of her hope into—suddenly opened, and there stood a girl, about fourteen, and when she saw them, she froze like a deer in the headlights.

She tried to go back into her room and shut the door, but Sarah put her foot in the way and asked her, "Are you Jesse?"

"How did you know my name? Who are you people? What do you want with me?"

"I'm a Detective with the Chico PD, and I know about you because we've been looking for you for over seven years. Are you ok? Have you been hurt? How long have you been here?"

"My name is Jesse, yes. I've been here for what seems like my whole life. How did you know I was here? Who's been looking for me?" It's a miracle they found her.

"I'll answer your questions once we get you out of here. Come with me. I'll take you out of here."

"I don't want to leave. There's been a nuclear bomb, and my whole family is dead except my father. He's been keeping me safe here. I don't want to die like the rest of my family. I'm not going anywhere."

"Look, Jesse, if there had been a nuclear bomb like your dad says, would we even know to be looking for you? Would we be trying to get you out of here? Your dad kidnapped you when you were just a little girl. He took you away from your mom and has been keeping you here against your will ever since. There was no nuclear bomb. Your mom has been worried sick since you went missing all those years ago. We're here to take you home. I know you're going to have lots of questions, and I'll do my best to answer them all, but for right now I want to get you out of here and to a hospital to make sure you are ok."

"I'm fine. I don't want to go. I don't believe you."

"When was that last time you were outside?"

"I don't know. It's been a while. That's why I don't believe you. He doesn't let me out of here, ever. He tells me it's safer for me to be locked up here then out there where I might die from the nuclear poison."

"He has you brainwashed, Jesse. There was no bomb. Can you try to trust me on this one?"

"No, I don't know you. Get out of my room. You've put a hole in the wall. Now that poison is going to seep in here and get to me too." She started to become a little freaked out, but Dave, who looked at Sarah, said to Jesse, "Listen, sweetie, would you believe us if you could talk to your mom?"

"What? How can I talk to my mom? She's dead."

"No, sweetie, she's not. I bet Officer Wheeler can get her on the phone for you."

"I sure can. Give me just a minute." Sarah walked away from Jesse's bedroom door to call dispatch so they could patch her through to the girl's mom.

"Hello, Shelly? This is Detective Wheeler from the Chico PD. I have some news for you. We've found your daughter, but she doesn't want to leave the house because she thinks you and her whole family have been killed by a nuclear bomb. Yes, ma'am, she's just fine. Listen, she won't come out of this house without talking to you first. Yes, yes, it's ok, please don't cry. She needs to hear your voice. Remember, she thinks you've been dead for the whole time she's been missing. Try to say something that only you and her know about. Ok, I'm going to give her the phone."

She handed Jesse the phone, and Jesse said, "Hello?" She listened for a couple seconds and burst out crying. "Is that really you, Momma? I thought you were dead. He told me you were all dead." She listened for a moment and then said, "Yes, Daddy."

Sarah had to choke back the tears, swallowing the lump in her throat, as she wailed for Jesse to finish her conversation with her mom.

Dave handed her phone back when Jesse was done, and Sarah asked her, "Are you ready to leave now?"

"Yes, I am. Do I have to talk to him when I leave?"

"No, sweetie, you don't. We are going to want you to give us a statement of what has been happening to you though. We can do that in a little while. Did you want to bring anything with you?"

"I don't want anything from that man," she said angrily through tears. "He's kept me here for so long, I don't even know what the sun feels like."

"I'm so sorry that you've had to go through this. We'll take you out the way that we came in, and you won't have to see your father," Sarah said with her arm around Jesse's shoulders.

"Please don't call him that. My father died when he put me in this room. The man that has kept me hostage for the last however many years is some lunatic."

When they reached the top of the stairs and they stepped outside, Jesse took in a deep, cleansing breathe. She looked around at everything and noticed how beautiful it all looked. Although this was where she had spent the last seven-plus years, she didn't remember what it had looked like when she was first brought here.

She breathed deeply again, and Sarah said to her, "I can honestly say that I know how you feel. I was also kidnapped when I was about the age you are now. It's very traumatic, and we will get you the help you need. For now, though, we're going to go get something to eat, go to the hotel and sleep, and then to the police station in the morning to get your statement. I know your mom is very happy that we found you and that you are ok. Are you hungry?"

"No."

"Ok, I just need to go tell my partner what's going on, and we can get going." Sarah put Jesse in her car with Dave to sit with her while she went into the house to let Brad know what was going on.

"Brad, we found her, locked in a room downstairs, no windows, no way to get out, locked in there like a caged animal. Mr. Sharpe, you are under arrest for the kidnapping and false imprisonment of a minor. You make me sick! How could you do such a thing to your own daughter? Telling her that her entire family is dead? I will do everything in my power to make sure that they throw the book at you. I don't care what it takes we will get justice for that little girl whose innocence you stole. Get this scumbag out of my face, cuff him, put him in a squad, and put him in jail."

"You haven't heard the last of me, Detective," he started to say.

"You need to be quiet until you're ready to give your statement. From what Jesse has already told us, I can see you being in prison for a very, very long time. Kind of fitting since you imprisoned your own daughter. Now she can return the favor. Get him out of here!"

One of the officers cuffed him, led him out of the house, and put him in a squad car.

As they took him away, Sarah said to Brad, "I told Jesse that she would be going back to her mom's tomorrow. I don't care what I have to do to make sure that happens, but since she's from Chico, she's going back. We can take a sworn statement from her and try not to traumatize this poor child any longer."

"I'm sure that since it started in Chico, it will be fine. If we run into any trouble, we'll get Layton involved. He's pretty persuasive when he has to be. The courts usually side with what's best for the welfare of the child, so let's just do what we have to for her right now."

"I did tell her she'd have to go give a statement at the station, and if I have to bring her in, I will, but I'd rather not. Let's ask Dave when we get in the car."

They walked to the car, and Sarah asked Dave to step out as Brad got in.

"Dave, can you call in CSI? Can you also tell me, do we really have to put her through a statement at the station tomorrow? Can't we do one at our station? She's already been through so much. I'm sure bringing her back to Chico isn't going to change what she has to say."

"I'm fine with it, Detective. I'll take the heat too if they want to blame anyone. She's pretty shook up over this whole thing. She hasn't stopped crying since we brought her out to the car."

"The poor thing. I can only imagine. This is why I want to take her back home. Maybe it won't be as hard on her there as it would be here, still away from her family. At least, going home, she can see them and know that they are actually alive."

"I agree. I'll stick around here and get this scene under control. We'll have CSI cover the whole house, top to bottom."

"Wonderful, thanks for your help with all of this. It's been a pleasure working with you."

They shook hands, and Sarah got back into her car as Dave walked back toward the house with the rest of the officers.

"Let's hit the road, shall we? Jesse, are you ok? Do you want to talk about it?"

"No, I don't want to talk about it. I'm just so incredibly angry and sad that my own father would do this to me. He is now dead to me. I hope I never see him again!" Tears started to run down her face even harder.

"I know this is difficult, but once we get back to Chico and we get your statement, you can start putting this behind you. For now, let's go to the hotel, order some room service, and get some rest."

Jesse put the window down while they were driving, loving the feeling of the breeze on her face and smelling the fresh air. Sarah looked at Brad and he at her. He reached over and squeezed her hand when he saw the tears in her eyes.

She swiped at them and said to Jesse, "How are you doing?"

"I'm ok, feeling a little bit better, I guess," she said, sniffling.

"It's going to take time for you to feel anything but anger or sadness. I think once you get to see your mom tomorrow, you might feel better than you do right now."

"I can't believe that my whole family isn't dead like he told me they were. How could he do this to me? What was in it for him? I still remember the day that he took me, like it was yesterday."

"Do you want to go to the station here and give your statement or when we get back to Chico? I don't know how you feel about talking about it, but if you want to get it over with, we can do it now. If you just want to talk about it and give your statement later, that's up to you."

"I don't know or care right now. I've been so lonely and afraid for so long that I don't think I have many other emotions. I was afraid that one day he wouldn't come back because he died from that nuclear gas as well. He had control over everything: what I watched on TV, the music I listened to, the clothes I wore, what I was taught, just everything. I'm so afraid to tell anyone what happened to me. I don't want anyone to hate me."

"No one will hate you, Jesse. You had nothing to do with this. You are innocent in everything except being a kid. You didn't ask for this to happen to you, and you didn't ask to be taken away from the rest of your family for so long. Everyone is going to be thrilled to see you and to see that you are doing well."

"I'm just so afraid still. I don't even know my own mother anymore. What's she like? Will she still love me? Does she think this was my fault? I have so many questions and no answers."

"Your mom was overjoyed when I called to tell her that we found you. She hasn't stopped loving you. She's been looking for you for seven years. She knows this wasn't your fault. It's the fault of that man who decided to take you away from her. Things will get better, trust me, Jesse. They did for me."

"Thank you for being so kind to me. I must sound like an absolute brat, whining about my life."

"Not at all! You sound like a very intelligent young lady that, with time, will be whoever she wants to be, and I think that person is going to be very special."

Jesse cracked a small smile, shut her eyes, and let the wind blow in her face. Once they reached the hotel, they ordered some food, called her mom to let her know they would be home tomorrow and that when they got there, Jesse would have to give her statement. Once they finished eating, they turned in because it was going to be another long day tomorrow. Sarah texted Nate to let him know that they found her, that she would be home tomorrow, and that she loved him and then she went to sleep.

29

IN THE MORNING the sun was shining brightly, and it was a beautiful day. They all got ready to go, and Sarah let Brad drive so if Jesse wanted to talk, they could. There wasn't much conversation on the way home, and Jesse barely took her eyes off the countryside as they drove back to Chico. It was a long drive, but once they got back to town, they went right to the station. Jesse's mom, Shelly, was there waiting for them. When they walked into the station, she was sitting there, tears already streaming down her face. A choked sob came from deep within her as she saw her baby for the first time in seven years.

"Oh my god, it's a miracle" she exclaimed as she stood up with her arms open wide.

"Mom? Is it really you?"

"Yes, baby, it's me."

Jesse ran to her mom, and they embraced and cried together. Sarah stood there with her own tears running down her face. Brad whispered to Sarah that he was going to go let the captain know they were back and that he would get a room ready to take her statement.

"Are you ok, sweetheart? Did he hurt you? You've gotten so big. You're so grown up now."

"I'm ok Mom. Nothing I can't handle. I'm still your little girl, and I always will be."

They hugged again, and Sarah cleared her throat.

"Why don't we go get this statement over with, and then your mom can take you home."

"You hear that, sweetheart? Home. You can come home. I never thought I'd say that. Thank you so much, Detective Wheeler. I am forever in your debt."

"Just doing my job, Shelly. You don't owe me anything. I'm just happy that we found her and were able to bring her back."

"I am very happy about that as well."

"Me too, Mom. I really like being able to say that again. I cried a lot when he first brought me to his house, thinking that you were dead."

"Let's not talk about that right now. Go ahead with the detective and give your statement, and then we can go home."

"Ok, I'm ready. Let's get this over with."

Brad had come back out, and they followed him to a room with a window, video camera, and tape recorder. Brad told Sarah to go ahead whenever she was ready. He went to the observation room instead of sitting in with them, thinking having a strange man in there might make her uncomfortable and unwilling to talk about what happened.

"Jesse, are you ready for this?"

"As ready as I can be."

"Ok, we can go as slow as you need to. I know this is going to be difficult to talk about, but you're safe now, and he will never hurt you again."

"Ok, I just want this to be over."

"What happened the day that he took you?"

"Mom and I had been at the grocery store, and she took me out of the cart while she loaded groceries when my dad pulled up in the lane behind the car. He got out, came toward me, and when I saw him, I ran over to get a hug. He put me in the car and drove away. I even dropped my favorite stuffed animal when he was there because it had been a while since I'd seen him. When I asked him where we were going, he said, just for a little drive. I fell asleep before we were ever done driving, and the next thing I remember is him carrying me into the house and putting me to bed."

"Were you downstairs when he put you to bed?"

"I don't remember if I was that night, but I do remember that when I woke up, I was in that place all by myself. I tried to get out the door, but it was locked. I started to cry, and I heard him tell me not to cry, that he'd be right in to see me. I have no idea where his voice was coming from, and I kept crying. He showed up within thirty seconds, picked me up, and dried my tears. I asked him when I could go home and see my mommy, and he told me the story about the bomb. Every time I asked him when I could leave, he told me the same story. My whole family was dead, killed by a nuclear bomb."

"How did he stop you from finding out the truth? There was a TV in your—let's call it an apartment."

"He controlled everything. When I was little, it was cartoons all the time and movies. When I started to get a little older, it was kids shows, no news, no way to know what was happening. I was a kid, what do I know about world events? I had a radio, but that only had one channel it would pick up, and there was never news on the radio either."

"Did he ever tell you why he took you?"

"He said he saved my life because the nuclear bomb was coming. I asked him once why he didn't save my mom, and he said because she wouldn't listen to him, so she was on her own. I cried for days after he told me that."

"Did he spend much time with you in your 'apartment'?"

"Not very much. He would bring me my meals and eat with me but then told me he had to work. When I was little, I never thought that it was strange that he would still be working after the bomb went off, but when I got older, I started to question some things, like how come he was able to live somewhere different than me, how come he could go outside, how did this bomb not kill him? He would put me off and change the subject, so I stopped asking."

"Did he ever hurt you?"

"When I was little, he wasn't mean, but as I got older, he got meaner. He used to slap me on the butt if he didn't like something I told him. I remember one time, I was trying to ask him why I had to stay down there still. It had been a few years since I'd been there, and he said, 'Stop asking me so many questions, you damn brat,' and he slapped me across the face. I decided that I wouldn't ask him stuff like that anymore. I didn't stop, though. I would get mad at him because I couldn't go outside. I didn't have friends, and I was so lonely. He called me a spoiled little brat who reminded him of my mother, and he took a belt to me. Afterward some woman came down and cleaned me up and told me that I should try to mind my manners and not make him so mad because then he wouldn't be mean to me."

"Who was this other woman? Did you ever get her name?"

"She did tell me her name once, and I think it was something like Shannon, Shari, something that started with an Sh. I didn't use her name, though. I called her CeCe, and I thought of her as like a second mom since mine was dead, or so I thought."

"Does Sharon sound right?"

"Yes, that's it. She was always very kind to me. She started to bring my meals to me. I saw less and less of him. When I asked her when I could get out of there, she said that was up to my father. I asked her if I could go outside, and she said that wasn't a very good idea because if my dad caught us disobeying, he's beat us both, so I never got to go outside in the entire time that I was there."

"What about school? You seem to be educated."

"Yeah, that was CeCe too. She told me that she had been an elementary-school teacher until her husband died. She lost her job because she couldn't make it through class without bursting into tears. I got to be very close with her. She shopped for all of my clothes. She would hug me when I was sad."

"Did your father see you every day?"

"No. There were weeks that would go by, and I wouldn't see him. He kept me down there and couldn't be bothered with me. Why would he do this to me? If he wanted me in his life so badly, why would he kidnap me and then leave me down there alone?"

"I can't answer for him, but I can make a guess. Your mom and dad were separated when you were kidnapped. I'm guessing he took you so that your mom wouldn't have custody. He was living all the way in Hollywood, and she was in Chico. She said that he was abusive to her and had started to be like that with you before you were taken. She wanted to keep you safe, and he just wanted to keep you, I think. What about other people? Did you see or hear anyone else while you were there?"

"No, him and CeCe were the only ones I ever saw besides whoever was on TV. I never heard anything except for what was going on in my 'apartment'. I had no idea who was coming to see me until I heard the door lock click."

"Did you ever try to escape?"

"I tried to run past him once when I was probably eight, but he spanked me so hard I couldn't sit down for a couple of days, and I could only sleep on my side. He always apologized for hitting me, and he said if I would stop making him so mad, he would stop being mean to me. I tried to be nice when he came to see me, but sometimes I was just so sad. He'd notice I'd been crying and ask me, 'What the hell are you crying about now, you big baby?' and that made me cry all the harder. I heard him mutter one day that he should have left me where I was instead of bringing me here, then he wouldn't have to give a shit about me."

30

Jesse had been crying for about an hour. Sarah asked if she wanted to take a break, and she said "No, I want to get this over with."

"Ok, let's keep going. What did he use to hit you with?"

"Sometimes his hand, sometimes a paddle, and of course, his belt. I know I have scars on my back because of that belt. When he would get mad and beat me with his belt, she would come down and put creams on the welts. I'd cry for hours, and she would hold me and tell me to try to not get into trouble so that I wouldn't get beaten. How was I supposed to know what would make him snap and want to hurt me? After a while, when he'd come in my apartment, I just didn't talk to him except to answer questions he asked. I stopped asking any of my own questions and just tried to get by day after day. I thought I would die down there. I even thought about killing myself just so it would all be over, but there was nothing sharp in there. I probably would have tried to use something on him so I could get out. I hated it there so much. I was always afraid he'd come down and be angry when he got there and beat me for no reason."

"Jesse, would you let me see your scars? I'd like to get pictures of them if that's ok with you?"

"Why do you need to see them? I'm going to have them the rest of my life, thanks to him."

"It's evidence against your dad to lock him up for a very long time. The more we have, the better it is for our side. If you aren't comfortable showing them to me, when we send you to the doctor for your physical, we'll get pictures of them then."

"Can we just do it all then? I really want to get through this and put it behind me."

"Of course, we can. Are you still doing ok? Do you need anything? Bathroom break, water, anything?"

"I would like to use the bathroom if that's ok? I could go for a glass of water too since you asked."

"Absolutely. Whatever will make this more tolerable for you. Right this way to the restroom." Sarah led her to the restroom and grabbed a bottle of water for her on their way back.

"Ok, are you ready to continue?"

"Yes, how much longer do you think?"

"I would say maybe another hour. Now, did you ever go to the doctor or dentist while you were there?"

"No, I was really sick this one time too. I was throwing up, had the chills and a fever, I laid on the bathroom floor all night just to be close to the toilet in case I needed to puke or poop. It was awful. When CeCe came down and saw me, she left right away, came down again, and had a bunch of medications with her. I don't know how long I was sick, but whenever I opened my eyes, she was there with me. She nursed me back to health and probably saved my life. He didn't check on me ever, so I would have died if she hadn't been there."

"I didn't see many toys down there. Were you allowed to play?"

"I had a bunch of toys when I was little, but whenever I made him mad, he'd take them away from me. He finally just never brought them back. He would take away things and then promise that he'd return them. He'd slap me and then say he'd never do it again. He was nothing but a liar, and I hope I never see him again."

Jesse started to cry softly again, and Sarah thought, *She's been through so much already. I need to wrap up this interview.*

"Jesse, can you think of anything else that you want to tell me?"

"Everything that he did to me he told me was for my own good. He touched me once in a very inappropriate place I found out later on when I told CeCe about it. She must have said something to him because he never did it again. I never heard anything. I'm guessing it was a soundproof place. He would come in with a nice tan and smell like outside, and he always told me it wasn't safe for me to be out there. He told me he had built up an immunity to the poison because he had been outside in it a couple of times, that's why he could continue to go outside. I asked him to take me outside with him once, and he shut me up by saying I might die, and did I want to die? I told him I didn't care anymore, and he slapped me across the face and called me an ungrateful little bitch. He said, 'I've tried to give you a good life, and all you can do is complain that you can't go outside. How about I take you outside and let you breathe in that rotten air and see how long it takes for your lungs to close up and for you to start choking to death. It's a slow and painful death, but if that's what you want, I'll let you go outside.'

"It scared me, so I never asked him again because I didn't want to die like that. I thought about what he said over and over again and wondered if that's how my family died. I believed anything he told me in the beginning because I had no one else to listen to. When CeCe started coming in his place, she wouldn't say anything about the bomb when I asked her. She said I'd have to talk to my father. You know, I never did ask her how she survived the bomb. She was the only other person I ever saw and thought that she was lucky to be alive like I was, but after several years of being there, I didn't feel lucky anymore. I felt sad. I didn't get out of bed for days sometimes. I didn't know what time it was, if it was light or dark out, or even what year it was. Once CeCe started coming on a regular basis, I asked her the date and time and began to keep track of it. I have journals that she brought me to put my thoughts into. I kept them hidden in my room so that he couldn't find them and use them against me. You'll find them in my closet under the third board from the back. CeCe helped me hide them in there. I'm so tired. Can I go now?"

"I think that we have enough for now. Once we retrieve your journals, they will probably be used as evidence against your father."

"I hope so. There is a lot of information in them about how awful he was. When I started to keep them, I would put in there how much I hated him hurting me, and I would pour my heart out. CeCe never asked if she could read them, and I know no one ever found them because I was never out of my room until you came to rescue me. I don't ever want to see them or him again if I don't have to."

"Are you ready to go home with your mom?"

"I never thought this would happen," Jesse exclaimed and started to cry all over again.

Sarah brought Jesse out to her mom, who shook Sarah's hand, wrapped Jesse in her arms, and told her, "Come on, sweetheart, let's get you something to eat and then go home."

"I can't wait to go home, Mom. I'm glad you never gave up on me."

"Never!"

They walked out of the station with their arms around each other, like they would never let each other go.

31

WHILE SARAH HAD been interviewing Jesse, Brad had been on the phone with Dave in Hollywood to let him know to arrest the house-keeper, Sharon. He also told him about the journals and where they could be found. Dave told Brad that Allan had lawyered up as soon as he was brought to the station, so they hadn't gotten anything out of him as of yet.

"Let his lawyer know that Jesse has told us all about her time with daddy dearest, and he will be going to jail for a very, very long time. He's done some pretty awful shit to that little girl, and if I were the judge, I'd throw the book at him and never let him see the light of day. Just like he did to her," Brad said angrily.

"I don't think I want to know what any of that is. Our officers have spent the better part of yesterday and again today at the house, combing through it to get any evidence that we can find against him."

"Those journals will help. Once you tell the lawyer about them, they may want to strike a plea deal, but I wouldn't settle for less than thirty years. That bastard has scarred that little girl physically and mentally something awful. You have to be a real psycho to do that to your own daughter. I would like to spare her the trial, but if they come at you with a ridiculous number of years for him to be in jail, I would like to ask her if she wants to take it to court or not. Don't make that decision without asking me first so I can ask her and her mom."

"I will leave that decision up to you, or I should say, up to Jesse. I still can't believe that all these years went by, and we had no clue that she was there, or at least we couldn't prove that she was there. Nice work on figuring it out, Brad."

"It wasn't me. It was all Detective Wheeler. She is the one that thought there might be other rooms in that house, and it turns out she was right. Did you guys find a way in from inside the house?"

"Yes, in one of the other rooms there was a staircase inside of a closet, and that's why no one knew that there was anything under the main living area. He sure is a piece of work."

"More like a piece of shit. Thanks, Dave, for everything and for assisting us with all of this. Let me know if he decides to talk or if he is going to remain silent. I'll talk to Sarah and see what she thinks about it going to trial."

"No problem, Brad. I'm just glad we found her alive and that we can hold him accountable."

"Amen to that. Bye."

"So long, Brad, nice working with you. Bye."

32

Brad hung up and went in search of Sarah, who was just saying goodbye to Jesse and Shelly.

"Hey, Sarah, got a minute?"

"Sure, Brad, what's up?"

"I just got off the phone with Dave, and her dad lawyered up and won't talk. I told him to arrest the housekeeper and where to find the journals. I also told him once he tells the lawyer what he has for evidence that they shouldn't settle for less than thirty years. What do you think Jesse and Shelly would say if they had to go to trial?"

"I know that they both don't want to see him again, but that being said, I know they both want him to pay for what he did to her. If it comes down to it, I would say they would go to trial, but we can cross that bridge if we come to it."

"By the way, you were great during this whole thing. You really showed me that you can handle yourself. I knew you'd be a great detective, but you went above and beyond for this little girl, and I couldn't be more proud of you."

Her face turned a bright crimson, and she said, "Ah, Brad, thanks! I knew we could do it. I knew we would find her and bring her home."

"We didn't, you did. I missed it all those years ago, and it took you a couple of weeks to figure it out. You will be a huge asset to this precinct. I bet that Layton is beaming about this one being solved, and in a positive way. Speaking of which, we should go and talk to him about this."

"Don't be so hard on yourself. If I hadn't been taken back in the day, I wouldn't have thought about secret rooms or anything like that. Who has that in their house anyway? It was a team effort, and I won't take all the credit for it."

They headed to the captain's office. He was on the phone and held up his finger for them to give him a minute. They waited outside of his office for him to hang up. Once he did, he motioned them into his office.

"Nice work on that kidnapping case. Matter of fact, that was the commissioner on the horn there, and he said that he is putting in for commendations for all of the officers involved with solving this one."

"I think that should strictly go to Sarah, Captain. She's the one that figured it out," Brad stated.

"No, Brad, it should go to all of us. We all worked hard at saving that little girl, and I'm glad that we accomplished our goal. I'm incredibly honored that you would want it to be just me, but that isn't how it works. The guys out in Hollywood also deserve the same thing. Captain Layton, will they also be recognized?"

"Yes, Wheeler, they will also be recognized. I must say that I'm really impressed with the work that you guys did on this case, what with it being a cold case and all. Do you have anything else for me?"

"Just to tell you that the suspect lawyered up right away and hasn't said a word about any of this to anyone. Sarah and I talked about it, and we think that if they try a plea that his jail time shouldn't be less than thirty years. Sarah thinks that if they tried for less than that, Shelly and Jesse would opt for a trial."

"I hope you're right, Wheeler. I'd like to see this guy put behind bars for the rest of his life. If it were up to me, he would be. I can't imagine how that little girl feels after being locked up alone for so many years. It really breaks my heart and pisses me off. Ok, if there's nothing else, I've got work to do."

"Us too. We've got a report to do on this case," Brad said.

Brad and Sarah left the captains office to go to their desks and do their reports.

33

WHEN SARAH ARRIVED home that day, if felt like she'd been gone for a month. To her surprise, the house was cleaned, she could smell food, and she could hear noises coming from her kitchen.

"Hello? Who's in there?" she asked cautiously.

"Welcome home, honey," exclaimed Nate as he poked his head out of the kitchen. "I'd come out and greet you, but I'm up to my elbows in here."

"Oh, thank God it's you, Nate. I was a little nervous there. But, thinking about it, would a burglar break into my house to make me dinner? Mm, whatever you're making smells fantastic."

She dropped her keys in the dish, kicked off her shoes, took off her gun, and went into the kitchen. She put her arms around Nate's middle and hugged him from behind.

He said, "How's my girl?"

"I'm doing great. I am on cloud ten after finding that little girl, Jesse, alive. Her father is a piece of shit and a coward. I hope they put him away for a very long time. What are you making?"

"I'm making some beer battered onion rings to go along with some jumbo prawns and fresh asparagus. Would you like to make us a couple of cocktails? I brought over the stuff to make mojitos."

"That sounds like a wonderful idea! Let me go get into my comfies, and I'll be right back." She went to her room to change and saw the bed was covered in rose petals. There were candles burning and soft music playing. She smiled, changed, and went back to the kitchen. "Hey, Nate, how on earth did I get so lucky to find you? You are one of the sweetest people I've ever met." She turned his head so she could give him a big, wet kiss and started making their drinks.

"Well, I aim to please, babe. It's really good to see you. It seems like you were gone for a month."

"That's funny that you say that. I thought the same thing when I came home."

"Great minds." He went to the sink and rinsed off his hands and said, "Now, come over here, and I can give you a proper greeting."

She walked over to him with their drinks and put them on the countertop behind him. He wrapped his arms around her and gave her a big hug and a very nice long kiss.

"I could get used to that kind of greeting," she said, a little out of breath.

"I could get used to giving that kind of greeting," he said, picking up his drink and holding it out for a toast. "To you and the team." They clanked their glasses together. "Congratulations on a job well done."

"Thanks, hon," she said as she blushed a little bit.

"Would you like to take a shower or anything before we eat? You have time. If not, you can tell me all about your exciting adventure."

"It definitely was exciting when we found her. To think that poor girl has been there for all of these years, and no one knew it except her dad and the lady he hired on to be her 'surrogate mother'. Her dad deserves everything he gets for what he's done. I was only missing for a short time, not years. I can't even imagine what she is going through, how she is processing this whole thing."

"I am so happy that you found her alive and well. Do you want to talk about it?"

"Do you really want to hear about it?"

"I do. If it's important to you, it's important to me." She started to tell him about the last couple of days. During her story, they ate, had another drink, and then went to the living room so she could finish her tale.

"That is incredible! You're right, though, what a piece of shit. Now, why don't you go take a shower, and I'll clean up the kitchen."

"I can clean up. You did cook after all."

"No, I insist. I'll clean up the kitchen. You go get cleaned up."

"Ok. Hey, Nate?"

"Yeah, babe?"

"I love you. It actually doesn't feel weird anymore when I say that."

He chuckled and said, "I love you too, and I'm glad it's not weird for you anymore. Now scoot."

34

SARAH WENT TO her room to get clean clothes and then to go in and take a long hot shower. Nate cleaned up the kitchen, made them both another mojito, and brought them with him into the bathroom. He stripped and got into the shower with her.

"Is this shower big enough for the both of us?" he asked as he stepped in.

"It's going to have to be, isn't it?" She turned around to face him and wrap her arms around him. They kissed and held each other.

"You feel incredible," he said.

"You feel pretty incredible yourself. Want to wash my back?"

"I'd rather wash your front," he laughed as she turned around.

"Maybe I'll let you do both."

"Sign me up for that job. Is it something that I can do on a daily basis?"

"Probably not, sweets, sorry." They let the water beat on their bodies as they stood, holding each other in the shower.

"Ok, time to get out. Water's getting cold, and I'm turning into a prune," she said reluctantly.

"Ok. I have a surprise for you when you get out, though."

"Oh? Whatever could that be?"

"You'll just have to wait for about fifteen seconds." He presented her with a towel and another drink.

"Oh, just what I wanted, to get dried off and drunk."

"Drunk? You're far from drunk."

"Keep feeding me these, and it won't take any time at all."

They dried off, and when Sarah went to put on her clothes, Nate said, "Um no, that won't do at all. The other surprise I have is in your room."

"I saw my room, and it's absolutely lovely."

"Glad you like it. Now follow me."

"If you say so."

They went into her room where they made love, long and slow.

"Wow, I could get used to this," she said sleepily.

"Really? How about moving in with me then?" he asked hopefully.

"I do like being with you, and tonight was sure unexpected and wonderful. You know what, what have we got to lose? Let's do it, let's move in together."

"Are you serious? That's great news! When is your lease up?"

"I think in October, but I'll have to check."

"This is the best news since you said you'd marry me."

"I'm beginning to like the idea a lot myself."

She reached for him again, and they made love again and then drifted peacefully asleep.

35

When Brad got home from the station that day, Lynda was waiting for him with open arms and a beer.

"I'm glad you're home, darling. How did it go? How are you feeling?"

"It's nice to be home, sweetie. It went great, and I feel amazing."

"Tell me all about it."

He started to tell her about the whole ordeal after a long pull on his beer. When he finished, he told her that everyone working the case was being given commendations for the job they did on the case.

"I still don't think it's right that Sarah doesn't get something special. She did an amazing job figuring this out."

"If I know my daughter, she doesn't want to be put in the spotlight. You all work for the same team, so you should all get some sort of credit."

"She said something like that too. The best news is that mother and daughter get to be a family again."

"That poor mother. How she must have suffered all these years. Seven years is a long time to wonder and worry about someone."

"You would have done the same thing for Sarah."

"You're right, of course. I guess it's just hard to give up when you don't have anything to say that you should. No body or no indication that she's been killed. I'm very happy for them. I'm also very happy you're home too. Are you tired? You've been out of work for a while now. How was it being back?"

"It was exhilarating. I didn't really think that I missed it that much, but when we were there and they were searching the house,

I was waiting for them to come and tell me if they found her, and it seemed like it took forever. Just by how long it took them, I figured she must have been down there. The look on Sarah's face when she came up to tell me and to address that pile of shit told me everything that I needed to know. I'm honestly so proud of her. She makes it look easy. She's going to go places if she keeps doing this."

"I'm so happy that she has you by her side while she does it. I can't think of a better person to help guide her and 'show her the ropes' of being a detective."

"Truthfully, she'll be able to show me a thing or two soon."

"Well, let's not go that far. She has a lot to learn, and I'm sure she will glean as much information from you as possible. Do you feel like grilling up some steaks? It's about time to throw them on."

"Sure, I'd love to, and I'd love another beer too."

"I'll grab the steaks and beer and meet you on the patio."

They went out to the patio where Brad put the steaks on the grill, put his arm around Lynda's shoulders, drew him to her for a nice long kiss, and said, "I feel so alive since being back on a case. It's the best thing in the world."

"I'm so glad for you. I was worried we'd never get to do anything like this again. It's all in the past now, so we can put it behind us and live our lives again."

Once the steaks were cooked, they went into the kitchen, where Lynda put the rest of dinner on the table, which consisted of baked potatoes with the works, crab salad, and garlic bread.

"Everything looks and smells terrific, and I, for one, am starved," Brad exclaimed.

"Me too. Let's eat."

After they finished dinner and the kitchen was cleaned up, Brad asked, "Do you feel like fooling around?"

"I really do, but are you feeling up to it? It's been a pretty exhausting couple of days."

"Not that exhausting."

He winked at her as he reached for her hand to lead her upstairs. They made love and drifted off to sleep.

36

THE NEXT MORNING at the station Sarah grabbed another of the cold-case files that she had in her drawer. She was reading it over when Brad walked in, and it looked like he had a spring in his step.

He had a huge grin on his face, which was infectious, and Sarah said, "You look like you're in an awfully good mood today."

"And why not? The sun is shining, the birds are singing, and I feel great. I am going to talk to Layton to see if I can come back full-time starting tomorrow. Today I am going to the doctor to tell him that I want to come back to work full-time. I didn't think that I was really going to miss this place that much after my attack, but after working with you for a couple of days, I really got the itch to get back to work."

"We do work well together."

"You, my dear, might just be the reason I want to come back so badly. You are going to do great things, and it inspires me to want to work with you. I've got the best damn partner on the whole force."

"I wouldn't go that far."

"Why not? It's true, and you should be damn proud of yourself for finding that little girl alive."

"We, we found her alive, all of us, not just me."

"Honestly, Sarah, why do you have to be so bullheaded? It was your idea, and it was stellar. Take some credit, will ya? They don't all work out like this. What have you got there, another case?"

"One of those cold-case files that you gave me. I don't feel like I deserve any more credit than anyone else that was involved with this case. You're the one who wouldn't give up on it. If you hadn't kept it with you, I would never have seen it, and then I wouldn't have ever had the idea I did. Can we agree that it was a team effort please?"

"What's eating you? I thought you'd be happy with the results of the case."

"Oh, I'm extremely happy about the way the case ended, but I don't think that you should make such a big deal about my part in it. I'm just doing my job."

"Ok, Sarah, I'm sorry. I'm just so proud of you and how you handled everything. I wanted to give you props. Anyway, I'm going to go talk to the captain."

"Will you stop by on your way to the doctor?"

"What is it? Do you need to talk to me now, or can it wait?"

"It can wait until after you talk to Layton."

"Ok, wish me luck."

"You won't need luck. The captain loves you, and so does everyone else. I'm sure he'll tell you that you can come back as long as you're cleared by your doctor."

"I sure hope so."

Brad walked to the captain's office, knocked, and walked in.

"Got a minute, Cap?"

"Yeah, what's up, Brad?"

"Well, I want to come back-full time. I'm going to the doctor today to get the all clear. Would you take me back full-time instead of part-time?"

"100% affirmative. It'll be damn good to have you back. If you're here tomorrow morning, I'll assume he said that you are good to go. If not, then whenever he says you can come back, I'll be good with that too."

"Thanks, Cap."

"No problem. Now get out of here. I've got work to do."

Brad walked out with an even bigger grin on his face.

Sarah saw it and said, "Let me guess, the cap said he's taking you back full-time?"

"Yes, he did. Now, what can I do for you? You don't seem as happy as I thought you'd be after yesterday."

"I am. It doesn't have anything to do with work."

"Oh? What's wrong? Is it Nate? What did he do? I'll wring his neck—"

Smiling, Sarah said, "Nate hasn't done anything, but it does concern him. He asked me to move in with him, and I said yes. Since we're getting married, we thought this would give us an idea on what it will be like. I don't know, though. I'm really not that excited about it today. Not like I was yesterday."

"What's changed since yesterday?"

"Nothing, but we finished having, well, you know, and he asked me to move in again, and I said yes, but today I'm having second thoughts."

"It might just be cold feet. From a man's point of view, moving in together isn't such a big deal, but I can see how moving in with Nate might cramp your style, a woman of the world such as yourself" he said with a twinkle in his eye and a smile on his face.

"Oh, Brad, c'mon, I'm being serious here."

"I'm sorry, I know you are, and I understand why you're a little nervous. This is your first real relationship, except for the shithead you were with when you were younger. If it makes you feel any better, Nate is a great man who thinks the world of you. Give it a trial run. If it doesn't work out, at least you'll know before you get to the 'I dos'. Don't sweat it, Sarah. It could turn out to be the best decision you ever made."

"Yeah, or the worst. I don't know. I'll have to see how things go. My lease isn't up until October, I think, so I've got some time. Thanks for listening and for your advice."

"Anytime. Well, I gotta run to the doctor. Maybe give your mom a call or stop by and see her, she might have better advice than me."

Brad left Sarah wondering still if she was doing the right thing. *Maybe Brad was right, I should call Mom.* She called her mom to see if she wanted to go out for lunch. She said yes, so they picked a spot and time, and Sarah went back to reading her cold case.

37

Sarah got to Pueblita's Mexican Grill before her mom did and was looking over the menu when she came in.

"Hello sweetheart, to what do I owe the pleasure of you inviting me to lunch?" she asked as she sat down.

"I need some advice."

"Oh?" she questioned with raised eyebrows. "What sort of advice do you need?"

"Well, I told Nate last night that I would move in with him an—"

"What? Oh, that's wonderful news, Sarah," she exclaimed after she interrupted.

"Well, I'm not sure how wonderful it is. I don't know if I'm getting cold feet, and I don't know if I'm doing the right thing. We haven't set a wedding date yet, and I don't know if I should move in with him now or not."

"And you thought you'd ask me for advice? I'm touched, honey. It's nice to be needed. I'm sure you two have stayed overnight together, right?"

"Well, yes," she admitted, her face turning crimson. "Everything is fine when we do, but I'm nervous that it will be too much of each other too soon."

Lynda laughed.

"Oh honey, it's natural to feel like that. I felt that way with both your father and Brad. Maybe you should try to spend a little more time together for the next couple of weeks and see if you can stand each other and then decide. What about going on a vacation together? You will be with each other all day every day. That should tell you if you can stand him or not. Really, Sarah, I think it will be fine. You agreed to marry him, so he must be a great person since you had basically sworn off men. Don't think too much about it. Tell him you'd like a 'trial' run and have some things at his place. You keep some of his stuff, and see what happens."

"Do you really think so? I'm so used to being alone and liking it that it might be hard for me to have him be there all the time."

"Why don't you two go on that weekend getaway you were going to take when Brad was hurt and see what happens?"

"I guess that wouldn't be so bad."

"You make it sound like a death sentence. Is there something about him that concerns you that you wouldn't want to do this? He seems like an outstanding young man who loves you deeply. What is it that scares you so much besides not enough alone time?"

"I love him too, and maybe it is that I won't have enough alone time, but maybe with my erratic hours, it will be ok. I don't find any faults in him yet, but what if I start, and what if I start to nitpick? Then what? He's a great guy, polite, caring, he cooks, he cleans, he's terrific, but what if I don't live up to his standards? What if I fall short of all of his hopes and dreams he's had for a wife and partner? I would hate to let him down like that."

"Sarah Wheeler, any man would be lucky to have you. You're passionate, caring, loving, sincere, and a list of other things a mile long. If he doesn't think that you would 'live up to his standards', he wouldn't have asked you to marry him. I still say, try the weekend getaway and then spend more time together before jumping in with both feet."

"Thanks, Mom, but you have to say nice things about me. You're my mom."

"I most certainly do not. If I thought there were things about you that some people might not like or find offensive, I'd tell you. Look, I love you, and I know you will make the right decision. Just know that if you do move in together and it doesn't work out, you can always come and stay with Brad and me until you find another place. I can even help you find one. Hey, I know. Why don't you talk to Nate about buying a new place instead of moving into his. This way, you guys can come up with your own living plans. I can even help you find the perfect house."

"Wow, that's a giant step from moving in together to buying a place together. It makes sense, though. Then if we can't stand each other, we can sell it, and if we can, then we can make our future there. It will also take a little bit to find a house, so that might be just what we need. See, this is why I called. I knew you'd come up with some good advice."

"Great, it's settled. Once you tell me to start looking for a place for you guys, I will. Now, can we order? I'm starving."

"Thank you, Mom. I really mean it too. You always know what to say to make it all seem like it's going to work out."

"Aw, Sarah, it's my job to make sure that my girl is happy."

"I'd say you're pretty darn good at your job too." Lynda blushed, and her eyes filled up with tears, and she mouthed a "thank you" to Sarah, unable to speak so as not to cry.

Once back at the station after lunch, Sarah texted Nate to see if he wanted to come over again tonight for dinner and a sleepover. She also told him he could bring some stuff over to keep there if he wanted to. He texted back that it was a date and a great plan.

38

SHE PICKED UP the file she had been reading before lunch and tried to start back where she left off but realized that she hadn't taken in any of the information because she had been worried about moving in with Nate. She started at the beginning, again. The case was an old murder case from the 80's a dozen suspects, no witnesses, inconclusive DNA results from the tests they had run back then.

She jotted down ideas as she went through the file and decided to take it home with her that night. Nate would have to understand that if she was going to solve these cases, sometimes she had to bring work home with her. She closed up the file, locked up her desk, and left for the day so she could get home and start dinner. She thought she would do something easy and stopped at the market to get the fixings for a homemade pizza. They'd had enough meals together for her to know what he would like and what he wouldn't. When he got there, she was in the kitchen, waiting for him and reading her file.

"Hello, beautiful," he said when he walked into the kitchen, giving her a kiss. "What are you doing?"

"Hi yourself, handsome. I'm reading through a cold-case file about a murder from the 80's. Dinner should be ready in about twenty minutes. Would you like a beer or a cocktail?"

"Not tonight. I've got some things I have to do tonight after dinner."

"Oh? Anything that you need help with?"

"No, it's for work. I have to get a bunch of equipment ready for a new job that I have to do in the morning. After dinner I've got to go back to the station to get it all together so I can go to the job right from home."

"You aren't staying here tonight?"

"I don't know what time I'll be done, and I'd hate to wake you up if it got to be too late."

"You don't need to worry about that. I'll be working on this file tonight, so if you want to come back, you can."

"I'll see how late it gets to be, and I'll text you to see if you're still up. What have you conjured up for us this evening? It smells great."

"I went simple and did a homemade pizza. It should be done in just a little bit. I was kind of hoping that we could talk a little bit about moving in together."

"Oh? Are you having second thoughts?"

"Not second thoughts, just a thought. What if we were to buy a house together? My lease isn't up until October, and I could move in with you then, and then when we find the perfect place, we could move in there."

"Why don't you just want to move into my place?"

"Because it's just that—'your place'. I want to find somewhere that will be our place. I want to find a place where we will both have our own spaces for stuff. I don't want a drawer in a dresser and no room for all of my things. What if we have a family some day? You said yourself that it's small, but it works for now. My mom would help us find the perfect place too."

"I like my house, though, Sarah. I really hadn't thought about getting a new place until after we were married."

"If we get one now, that's one less thing we have to do after we get married. You don't need to tell me tonight. Think about it for a few days and let me know."

"Ok, I'll think about it."

Sarah was confused as to why there was push back on getting a new house. Maybe he's having second thoughts about moving in together. She went to the oven, checked the pizza, and set the table for them.

"Ready to eat?"

"Huh, what? Um, yeah, sounds good."

"Is everything ok, sweetie? You seem distracted."

"What? Oh, no, everything is fine. I'm just going through the list of things I need to pick up for that job tomorrow."

"So where is this job you're doing?"

"I, uh, can't tell you right now. It's classified for right now."

"Very secretive," she said with a smile on her face.

"Look, my job is like yours. I can't tell you about everything. You don't hear me asking you twenty questions about your file. Don't ask me about this anymore."

"What's wrong? I was just joking around. Lighten up, for crying out loud."

"Sorry, I just don't need the third degree about what I'm doing all the time. You know what, I'm just going to go get this done now. I'll talk to you later."

He got up and walked out of the kitchen and out of her apartment.

What in the hell is wrong with him, and why did he get so upset about whatever job he's doing tomorrow? Oh well, more pizza for me. She took the pizza out, cut it up, and ate alone. When she was done, she cleaned up the kitchen, went to the door and put the chain on it, and sat in the living room and finished reading her file. She had a list of questions, ideas, and theories that she would start on at the office tomorrow.

Since she didn't think Nate was coming back, she took a long hot shower and went to bed early. She thought that if he did come back and tried to get in with his key that the chain was on the door, and it would serve him right for being such a jerk. *What in the world did I say that made him jump down my throat? I can't worry about it, but if this is what living together was going to be like, then I want no part of it or marriage.*

She decided that she would talk to him about it one more time, and if he didn't apologize for being a dumbass, then she would have to take a long hard look at their relationship. She drifted off to sleep, hoping that he was just nervous about the job he was supposed to do and not something else. Unsure of what that was, she slept. In the middle of the night someone tried to get into her place but was unsuccessful. Sarah never heard or knew a thing about it until morning.

When she got up in the morning, she got ready for work and opened her door to leave when she found a dozen roses on her door-step. She picked them up, smelled them, and looked for a note. There wasn't a note, but she was pretty sure she knew who they were from. She took them back into the apartment, put them in some water, and headed to the station. She'd have to thank Nate when she saw him.

39

WHEN SHE GOT to the station, Brad was already at his desk, looking through a file.

"Hey, Brad, good morning. I'm so glad you're back."

"Good morning, partner. Damn glad to be back too."

"What's on our agenda today? Is that a new case you have there?"

"No, it's an old cold case."

"Really? I read through another one that you had given me, and I have a list of questions and other stuff that maybe we could go through today?"

"Sure, we can. Which case is it?"

"It's a murder from the 80's. The first thing I'd like to do is see what you remember about it. The second thing I'd like to do is go through the evidence box and see what's still in it. If there's still things we can run new DNA tests on, I'd like to do that as well. There was so little information in the file I can see why it went cold. It might be harder than normal to find a witness now after all of these years, but I'm willing to try if you are."

"I like the way you think. Let's get to it and see if we can close another one."

"I just have to text Nate quick. He was being weird last night, and I found a dozen roses on my doorstep this morning, and I wanted to thank him for them."

"Ok." Brad went back to reading his file while Sarah texted Nate.

Even though she knew he was on a job, she didn't want him to think that she didn't appreciate the flowers. What she got back from him was outrageous.

His text said, "Those flowers weren't from me. They must be from your other lover. I came back to apologize for being a jerk and saw them lying in front of your door. There was no note, so I wasn't sure who I was supposed to hate. Really, Sarah? Someone else is leaving you flowers? Why did you bother to get engaged to me? I tried to get in too, but the chain was on the door. I guess you were trying to keep me out so I wouldn't catch you and this mystery man. Maybe you'd just be happier if we didn't see each other anymore. I thought we were going to be so happy too. Maybe this was too soon, but I thought you were the one."

Her jaw dropped, and she gasped at what he had to say. She couldn't respond right away because she was floored. Brad asked her if she was all right, and she said no and handed him her phone.

After he read it, he gave a low whistle.

"Who do you think those flowers are from?"

"I have no idea. You know that Nate is the only one I've dated since Luke. This is awful. What do I do now?"

"You'll have to tell him that you have no idea who they are from. You were alone last night—you were alone, weren't you?"

"Of course, I was! I put the chain on because he was being a jerk, and I didn't want him coming back in the middle of the night."

"Tell him that."

"I can't believe that after everything, he would even suspect that there is something going on with me and someone else."

She chose her words carefully when she replied, "I don't know who those flowers are from. Obviously, if I knew they weren't from you, do you think that I would thank you for them? Do you not know me at all? You're my first and only, Nate, and I am in disbelief that you would think that I would sleep with anyone else while being engaged to you. I don't know what is going on with you, but if you don't want to see me any longer, that's fine, but don't accuse me of something unless you have facts to back it up." She was flabbergasted that he would think that she would sleep with someone else.

What has gotten into him? she wondered.

She didn't think that he was there and so was floored when he came upstairs and tapped her on the shoulder and asked, "Can we talk?"

"I think we better before this gets out of hand." They went to a conference room and shut the door.

"I'm sorry, Sarah. I freaked out when I saw those flowers, and then when I couldn't get in because of the chain being on the door, I jumped to conclusions and I—"

"Stop right there, I don't know what has gotten into you the last couple of days, but I will not stand here and let you accuse me of such things. I haven't ever been with anyone, and it was a huge leap for me to sleep with you. How dare you think such awful things about me! I said that I'd marry you because I love you, and I thought you loved me too. Maybe you're right. Maybe it was too soon to get engaged, but I'll be damned if I'll let you drag my name through the mud."

"Are you finished?"

"Yes, for now."

"As I was saying, I realized after getting your text that I was wrong. I trust you, and I do love you, and I want to marry you. This job I'm doing has me paranoid, and I took it out on you. I'm sorry. Will you forgive me?"

"I'm pretty steamed at your right now. Maybe you should go do your job and stop back and ask me when you're done with it. I think I need some space to figure out if I can let go of what you said."

"I really am very sorry. I have a way of jumping before looking. I'll give you some space. I love you."

He walked out of the room and shut the door quietly. Sarah took some deep, calming breaths and went back to her desk.

"Everything ok?" Brad questioned.

"Um, he apologized, but I didn't forgive him just yet. I told him to go do his secret job and that I needed some space. I honestly can't believe what he said. He said he tends to jump before looking, but this was seriously uncalled for. What do you think?"

"I think he has a jealous streak. Maybe the flowers were meant for a neighbor, and the person had the wrong apartment. Let's hope to God that you aren't being stalked again. If that's the case, you will be moving in with your mother and me. I won't take no for an answer. We have the security system and a room all ready for you. I think we need to find out where those flowers came from."

"I agree, and that's just what I'm going to do." She got up and looked at him and asked, "Are you coming, partner? We've got a mystery to solve."

"We certainly do. Let's go."

40

THEY DROVE BACK to the apartment building and started knocking on doors to try to find out who left flowers for someone. There were quite a few people that weren't home, so Sarah decided to draft a note and hang it by the mailboxes. The note said, "Found one dozen roses on my doorstep. If they were meant for you, please come and pick them up at #217."

"There, hopefully, that will do the trick," she muttered.

She and Brad headed back to the station to work on that old murder case. Once back at the station, she couldn't concentrate, and she told Brad she was going home for the day and work on some other ideas for the case.

"Now, Sarah, don't go into a funk. I understand that you've had a fight with Nate, but it shouldn't affect your day."

"Well, it does, and I'm going to get to the bottom of this."

"Ok, you go home, and I'll look over what you have so far on this old case. Let me know if something turns up."

"I will," she promised.

Once she got home, she was still so irritated she decided to soak in a bath to relieve some of the tension she was feeling. She was just getting out of the bathtub when there was a knock at the door.

She threw on her bathrobe and called out, "I'll be right there." She went to the door and looked out. There was a woman standing out there with her note in her hand. She asked through the door, "Can I help you?"

"Yes, I think you have my flowers."

"Oh, yes, of course, just a second." She unlocked the door and opened it. She asked the woman to come in, apologized for being in her robe, and said, "I'll be right back with them."

"I'm really sorry about the mix-up. I just started dating a new guy, and he asked me if I got the present he left for me, and I was like, 'What present,' and he said, 'The flowers.' When I saw your note, I figured they must be for me."

"No problem. Here you go. What apartment do you live in?"

"I live right down the hall in #219. Thank you for putting up the note. They are beautiful."

"Yes, they are, and it's not a problem. My fiancé was thinking that I had someone else in my life when he saw them on my doorstep."

"I hope it didn't cause any problems."

"Oh, none I can't handle. My name is Sarah by the way."

"Oh, hi, I'm Chris," she said as they shook hands. "Well, I'm going to get back to my place and put them in some water."

"Nice to meet you, Chris. You must be new to the building?"

"Yes, I moved in a little over a month ago."

"Welcome! I hope we run into each other again."

"Me too. Thanks again. Bye."

"Bye," Sarah said and shut the door.

Well good, mystery solved. She decided to let Nate off the hook but texted Brad about the flowers first so he wouldn't worry about her.

She texted Nate next and said, "I forgive you for being a jerk. The flowers were meant for my neighbor in 219. Do you want to come over later?"

She wasn't expecting a response right away, but he texted her back and said, "If it's ok, I'm beat, and I'm just going to go home tonight. I'll see you in the morning, though. I love you."

That was fine too. She texted him she loved him and sat on the couch until late, going over that file again. When she headed to bed, it was close to one in the morning. Hopefully whatever is going on with Nate will be better soon. She knew she couldn't deal with all this drama all the time.

When she laid down, she couldn't fall asleep, so she thought she'd go for a run. It had been way too long since she went out running, but it was going to feel great to stretch out her muscles and get some exercise. She put on her running clothes, her holster, headphones, and went for a run. She returned about two, felt exhilarated, and hit the shower. She thought, *I should do that more often. It felt great.* Once out of the shower, she went back to bed and fell fast asleep. She had no way of knowing how a chance meeting would forever change her life.

ABOUT THE AUTHOR

MARY LIVES IN northern Minnesota and enjoys reading, gardening, cooking, fishing, crocheting, and writing. She enjoys time spent with family and friends and loves to snuggle and play with her dog. She enjoys new experiences with the ones she loves. She believes that no matter your age, never stop hoping and dreaming, because then you'll have nothing to aspire to. If you have nothing to aspire to, you stop living.

CPSIA information can be obtained
at www.ICGtesting.com
Printed in the USA
LVHW021032190921
698186LV00001B/41